Seasons
of the
Heart:

3 NOVELLAS

Seasons of the Heart:

3 NOVELLAS

EDWARD K. MACKENDRIK

Happiness & Heartache

Traveling from state to state and job to job, trying to decide what to do, where to do it, and who Arthur Haley wanted to do it with was a real challenge. Arthur Haley was a healthy man standing seventy-six inches tall and weighing two hundred and ten pounds. He was athletic, enjoyed different sports and usually bowled in the top two hundred range. He was an ambitious man wanting to achieve significant accomplishments.

Arthur Haley joined the U. S. Navy where he spent four years as an air traffic controller but became impatient with the pay scale and did not reenlist for a second tour. He had received outstanding reviews as an air traffic controller and was well respected by fellow Navy air traffic personnel. His commanding officer promised a promotion upon reenlistment, however, Arthur had heard Navy promises before and declined.

Memories of his beloved father and mother weighed heavy on his heart. His mother had died two years earlier, and his father just six months ago. Both times, Arthur grieved more than he thought he should. He requested extended leaves of absence each time, and visited their graves often.

Returning to the Navy, he dedicated himself to learning more about death and dying, and about the grieving process. During discussions with Navy Reenlistment Personnel, he refused, again, to reenlist and requested an early release to return to civilian life. Three weeks later he was discharged and left The Great Lakes Naval Air Center as a free man.

Once again, he traveled to his home in Oklahoma and visited the family grave. Consistent with the information he had been reading, he again committed to knowing more about the grieving process and began to focus on some of the things he had dreamed about while aboard ship in the Pacific.

When he considered getting reacquainted with people whom he had known in the past, Arthur thought of Abigail Henderson, an attractive young lady he had dated while in high-school. Since graduating, they had always stayed in touch. He suggested they meet for an early afternoon cup of coffee, and Abigail responded enthusiastically.

They enjoyed their time together and spent several hours renewing their experiences over the past four years. This led to a courtship and discussions about careers and future plans.

When Arthur noticed an advertisement from the Federal Aviation Administration (FAA) for air traffic controllers, he submitted an application for one of the positions. With four years of experience and a degree in business management, which he earned while in the Navy, impressed them, and he was hired for duty at Fort Wayne Air Traffic Control Tower, in Indiana.

Arthur was thrilled at the news. Abigail was less enthused. Even though she was single and employed part time, she was committed to living in Tulsa—her home town. Arthur appreciated Abigail's values, but he found it difficult to understand her reluctance to relocate. He continued to surface the subject during the three weeks until his report date, and the thought of Abigail lingered in his head.

On the date of his departure, Abigail became very emotional and asked if she could visit him in Fort Wayne. This gave him a small amount of hope. He would continue to pursue Abigail, and made good-bye promises.

Her reluctance bothered Arthur for another reason. He knew he was not going to be in Fort Wayne any longer than it took him to negotiate a transfer to a larger facility where the air traffic was heavy and complex and the pay was greater. He wanted a challenge, and he was willing to work for it. But this would mean moving more than once.

In 1972, Arthur reported for training to the FAA Aeronautical Center in Oklahoma City, Oklahoma. He applied himself toward learning the way civilian air traffic controllers performed their tasks as well as the rules and regulations that governed their decisions. In just a few months, he met the qualifications for certification with the highest grade point average ever at the center. With this achievement on his record, Arthur began to think about his career at Fort Wayne. He noticed an article in the publication FAA World, and he kept a copy for later use. He also knew that his best chance for promotion in the field was to combine his technical skills with his natural ability to be well-mannered and kind.

During a social gathering attended by many of the air traffic control students, Arthur met a beautiful lady—Carlee Jenkins, from Albuquerque, New Mexico. Carlee had the most beautiful smile he had ever seen, and her eyes were difficult to describe and even more difficult to leave alone. He caught himself looking at her eyes even when he didn't need to. He told himself not to stare, but that was even more difficult. Dancing with Carlee was the most enjoyable time Arthur had ever had.

During casual conversations at dinner that evening, Arthur asked, "Where do you expect to be assigned upon completion of your training?"

She replied, "I am being assigned to the Control Tower at Albuquerque, New Mexico."

Disappointed, Arthur said, "I am going to Fort Wayne, Indiana."

They exchanged address information and phone numbers which led to a long and involved friendship.

Over the next few years, Arthur and Carlee kept in contact, occasionally meeting half way for a casual weekend of dancing and great conversation. They allowed only thirty minutes each of shop talk as, otherwise, they would both consume the entire weekend with war stories and experiences.

In a letter Carlee had sent, she wrote that she was tired most of the time and planned to see her doctor to determine the root cause. Arthur responded via letter saying he was going to transfer to the busiest and most complex air traffic control facility in the FAA—O'Hare Control Tower in Chicago. Carlee wrote back asking if he thought she could get certified at the same facility. Arthur wrote a simple note that read, "Sure thing."

Without much discussion, Carlee submitted a bid for the same facility where Arthur was planning to work. The transfer was approved, and she was assigned to a team of controllers that occasionally, but not consistently, worked with Arthur. Her training was effective, and she certified quickly and was transferred to the radar function to begin training.

Carlee certified on two departure control functions and began training on Arrival Radar functions. She began to feel ostracized by other women in the facility by their comments about her reluctance to have sexual affairs with male controllers.

Still feeling weak at times, Carlee scheduled an appointment with her physician and learned she had Multiple Sclerosis (MS).

Carlee kept this information to herself. Unfortunately, the secrecy contributed to further alienation by the other women in the facility. She seldom participated in small talk, including those who had achieved full certification. Occasionally, Carlee would seek out Arthur. The two seemed to have a lot in common and enjoyed their time together.

As the months passed, Carlee worked the departure control positions while she waited her turn on the final two arrival radar positions. They were the most difficult to learn and apply consistently. In the midst of training for these, Carlee began to feel weaker and weaker. She never complained and continued to learn and apply the necessary skills for certification.

One afternoon, during a heavy session on an arrival radar position, Carlee was training when her instructor yelled at her.

"Cunt!" he said at one point.

She lost control of her emotions. "Seriously? Well, get this picture," she yelled and gave him a vulgar gesture as she was leaving. She stormed out of the control room and proceeded to look for the manager of the facility. When she did not find him, she informed her immediate supervisor that she was taking sick leave and was going to see her doctor.

Arthur was not aware of Carlee's conflict with her instructor. He was no longer associated with the control tower. Carlee looked but failed to find him, and she did not have a forwarding address or phone number to leave for him.

Carlee did not return to the facility. She was too embarrassed. She did keep the doctor's appointment, and he explained her MS diagnosed and what it meant for her career—a death sentence to the Class II Physical required by all in the profession. Carlee was withdrawn from the eligibility list for controller positions anywhere. She cried and cried for days.

She contacted administration at the facility and applied for the FAA Second Career Program. Leaving the facility was a brave move for Carlee. She began to realize just how much she was on her own.

What Carlee did not know was that Arthur had also failed to pass his Class II Physical exam. The FAA Regional Flight Surgeon had classified him as medically disqualified to perform the Air Traffic Control function. Troubling him most was the way the FAA had handled the recent DL42/SC 91 crash. He was well acquainted with the supervisor on duty in the control tower on the night of the crash on Runway 27. The National Transportation Safety Board (NTSB) and FAA found the controller, who was working the Ground Control Position at the time of the accident, at fault for not using the correct phraseology when instructing DL42 to "Just pull over to the 32 run-up pad, and let me know when you have a gate assignment." Proper terminology would have been "DL42, use the runway 32R run-up pad, and inform me when you have a gate assignment." That ground controller ultimately made poor decisions in life, as well, and lost his wife and child. He spent time recovering in a mental institution.

The FAA held the supervisor on duty that fateful evening as responsible for the accident. The Airport Surveillance Display Equipment (ASDE), which was inoperative, was never mentioned. The punishment for the supervisor in the control tower was of an administrative nature. He was relieved of supervisory responsibilities. That supervisor resigned his position and retired from Federal Service.

This event weighed heavily on Arthur, and the refusal of the Regional Flight Surgeon to approve his Class II Physical pushed Arthur toward the Second Career Program. He was approved. Though this provided him a bump in income, it did not assuage his pride. The work was not challenging. He became emotionally lost. For the next ten years, he searched for Carlee—the only girl he had ever loved.

Because of the overwhelming frustration Arthur experienced, he gave serious thought to returning to Oklahoma. His initial reluctance stemmed from the fact that Oklahoma would bring back the emotional loss of his father. He wondered if he could handle that in addition to his longing for Carlee.

"Get a grip," he told himself. "I'm not giving up on finding Carlee."

***

Everything Carlee tried caused her significant internal turmoil and serious doubts about her abilities. This feeling continued to haunt her until she had mastered whatever the most recent project was. Then she blossomed with excitement and jubilation.

While she had worked as a controller, she overheard several of the other women talking about having sex with the male controllers. She asked herself numerous times if she should also participate as it might improve her not so good relationship with the women and perhaps they would stop teasing her about remaining celibate, but she could not bring herself to experiment and remained the topic of conversation among the women controllers.

Carlee's father tried on several occasions to find out what was bothering his daughter and what she needed, however they failed to communicate effectively, and their relationship deteriorated to an ugly state resulting in less communication and hurt feelings. Trying almost anything to improve her relationship with fellow controllers, Carlee accepted a date with one of the male controllers and they spent the weekend in a motel. She later described her experience as awful.

Embarrassed by her experience over the weekend, Carlee became even less communicative than before. She began to experience difficulties performing in training, and her instructor yelled at her and called her a cunt. Carlee immediately unplugged from the operating position and stood up to leave the flight room (IFR). She wanted to talk to Arthur.

Maintaining a stoic exterior, she walked to the personnel office. The manager let her know that Arthur had been approved for the second career program and had departed the facility a month earlier. He left no forwarding address or phone number.

Carlee felt sick. She did not know if it was from missing Arthur or from her MS, but she made another medical appointment. The doctor—in coordination with the FAA Regional Flight Surgeon—withdrew Carlee's physical. The personnel manager informed her of the Second Career Option and told her she could no longer work live air traffic. After some consideration, she accepted entry into the program at Regional Headquarter in Des Plaines, Illinois.

She asked about Arthur, however they refused to give her his contact information.

Disheartened, Carlee went home realizing she had her income but no pride. She opened a beer, then two, and then forgot how many more.

Carlee called a couple of her friends, but when they found out she was medically disqualified to work and was essentially out of a job, they ignored her. Carlee began to seriously worry about her future.

***

Arthur and Carlee had been good friends, but neither thought they were in love, they just respected each other. Once, ten years earlier, they had attended a Cubs-White Sox game. Arthur had never forgotten the kiss Carlee gave him when their evening came to an end. He also never forgot the color of her eyes and her beautiful smile. He had searched for Carlee, moving to the state of Idaho when he heard that she had moved there.

One evening, out of desperation, Arthur tried again to locate Carlee and to tell her he was in Mountain Home, Idaho near where he thought she lived. When he called, Carlee was surprised to hear his voice. She was anxious to see him and wanted to catch up on ten years of lost friendship. Arthur suggested they meet at a restaurant of her choice.

Carlee identified one similar to the one they sometimes ate lunch at in Chicago. While waiting, Arthur became anxious. Would he remember her as she was in Chicago, or would he recognize her as she now was? He wondered if she was in a relationship.

Arthur realized the thirty minutes had passed, and he had not seen anyone resembling Carlee. He began to lose his confidence just as a late model convertible stopped at the curb and Carlee Jenkins stepped out. They hugged for a long moment.

Arthur said, "You look great!"

Carlee waved her driver goodbye, and they both realized that, even though they were in a crowd of people, they were alone.

"It's been ten years," she said. "We have a lot to discuss."

They entered the restaurant, and the hostess directed them to a table near the back of the room. During the meal, the two realized that they often held hands. Arthur could hardly speak as he was trying to convince himself this was real.

Reading his mind, Carlee assured him, "This is real. It is our time."

Arthur liked the way she talked—her words, her voice, her tone. He could hardly believe ten years had passed. Not only had they lost complete communication with each other, but they had also lost their way.

Arthur looked Carlee in the eyes and said, "We must go somewhere private and cover the times we have lost."

Carlee looked at him and smiled. "I will go wherever you want."

They finished their meal and went to Arthur's place. He could not contain his happiness as he kissed her lips and her hands. Arthur looked at her beautiful eyes and terrific smile. They held each other as if they were fearful of losing each other again.

"Tell me about the last ten years," Arthur said, "and I will listen."

She told him everything.

When it was his turn, he told Carlee, "I need to do something important before I begin to tell my side of this sordid picture."

Carlee asked, "What do you need to do?"

Arthur carefully placed his arm around Carlee and hugged and kissed her for a long while. In between kisses, Arthur muttered, "How happy I am to be holding you. I promise to never, ever separate from you again."

When she smiled, Arthur realized her smile and her eyes were almost more than he could handle emotionally.

"Carlee," he began when it was his turn, "you may recall I was selected for a first level supervisor position. Those individuals who had bid on the same job were upset and, at first, they did some crazy things when they worked for me. After a couple of months, things began to work smoothly again.

"After the sick-out plan stopped, most of the Professional Air Traffic Controllers Organization (PATCO) members continued to encourage sick-outs to protest FAA policies. As you may recall, I refused to participate and walked out of the union meeting."

Carlee nodded her head.

"I became an unhappy camper," Arthur continued. "The stress level increased to unbelievable levels. My car was keyed from front to back. Shortly after that, I lost my Class II Medical, and this disqualified me from controlling live air traffic. I left the facility. Life has been a hell hole for me ever since.

"I traveled across this country—in the south during cold weather months and in the north in summer or warm weather months. I was like a lost puppy, going from town to town wondering what I was, who I was, and what was I going to do. I do not want to talk about the bad years, which were many, but I always thought of you, Carlee, and your beautiful eyes and smile. Every time, my spirits lifted.

"There were times when I went to church, and I do not remember the name, but they sang songs like The Old Rugged Cross and a Willie Nelson song, *Why Me Lord*. When I heard them, I cried and asked God to direct me to you. Now, here we are, just the two of us, and I am holding you close." He smiled at her. "Now that we are together, I want to plan a life for the two of us."

Carlee pulled away for a moment. "Are you sure you want to build a life with me?"

"What could keep us apart now?"

Carlee leaned into Arthur's shoulder and began to cry. "I cannot talk about it," she sobbed. "I don't think you want a commitment with me."

"Please," he said. "Tell me what's wrong."

Carlee dried her tears and said, "That was my sister who drove me here. She drives me wherever I need to go. I cannot get a drivers' license due to my Multiple Sclerosis (MS) and what it does to my central nervous system."

Arthur held her tight. "We can overcome all obstacles, regardless of the complexity and regardless of how long it takes. We will prevail. Do you love me?"

"Yes, I have loved you for years! I just didn't know where you had moved to."

Arthur looked in Carlee's eyes and said, "We are going to be a happy couple."

"We need to talk about my problems," she said, pulling away again. "You need to understand the needs they create."

"Where do I go to learn about MS?" he asked.

She looked astonished. "You are the first person to ask me that question. I will get the answer. I think it is the Mayo Clinic in Rochester, Minnesota." Carlee then told Arthur, "I live in a rented apartment about two miles from the restaurant where we ate. It's set up for my special needs."

Arthur nodded. "I need to make some changes in the way I live," he said, "and it is important that we discuss our future together. My past has been awful. I have done things for which I am ashamed. We must be honest with each other and not hide anything the other one needs to know in order to make good decisions affecting our lives. For example, do you care if I have had sex with other women?"

"Yes, I care."

"Can you travel with me?"

Carlee looked concerned. "Maybe."

"Can you eat what you want?"

"No," she said, shaking her head. "I am severely restricted and must follow my diet every day."

Arthur said, "Can we plan ahead and schedule a trip to the Mayo Clinic?"

"Perhaps. But I have a doctor appointment in two days."

Arthur quickly asked, "Can I attend the doctor appointment with you?"

"Yes," Carlee said.

They talked long into the night.

When Arthur promised to tell her everything she wanted to know about his life, they held each other tight again. He kissed her and asked, "Will you marry me?"

Carlee cried and said, "Yes," but then she frowned. "I have to explain. Arthur, I am not supposed to live for more than five more years."

"That is five more years than I knew about yesterday, so let us make the best of it." They hugged again.

"How long is your lease?" he asked after thinking about something.

"It's month to month. Why?"

Arthur said, "I want to go to the doctor with you, and then let the two of us decide our next step."

***

Carlee wanted Arthur to meet her sister Eileen, so they made reservations at the restaurant that served seafood, steak, and a Mexican food.

Arthur asked, "Which diet are you on today?"

"Fish," Carlee said.

Arthur then said, "Carlee, I need for you to fill me in on the ten years we lost."

Carlee looked at her sister said, "After dinner."

After they finished their meal, Eileen excused herself to let the couple catch up on their own. "I'll see you at home," she told Carlee.

Following dinner, Carlee began by telling Arthur, "I left Chicago in 1967 after some very difficult years following my air traffic job. I had to deal with myself and my ego. I felt so horrible that I did not complete a certification process." She shook her head. "It was mainly due to the instructor. He called me a dirty name. After several years, I still woke worrying about it only to be subjected to it again in my sleep.

"I was certified on three radar positions. I don't know why the supervisors allowed the on-the-job training instructors to insult and demean me merely because I made a mistake and was in the process of correcting it. I thought it then and I think it today. I've never heard any of the competent instructors berate their students or call them nasty names; only the incompetent ones who had to fight to keep their job because of their poor performance." Her shoulders sagged. "In the end, it did not make any difference because my failing to pass the class II physical was the killer.

"After that, I left the facility, said good-bye to a fabulous career and walked into the cold Chicago wind to brave seeking new employment. I walked the streets of Des Plaines where I lived, but I was not content with anything I did. Most of it was menial stuff without challenge or reward. No self-satisfaction. My health did not help. I was aware of the deterioration and the ultimate possibility of disability.

"I had a male friend who said he would help me." She rolled her eyes. "That lasted for two days. Just for the record," she said, trying to reassure Arthur, "my boy-friend and I were merely that—friends. Nothing more. We seldom kissed and, when we did, it resembled a brother and sister kissing. No passion. I found myself alone with no job, and no friends. I was lonely. Because of my health, I decided to go back home to Albuquerque and live with my parents.

"I quickly noticed I had no friends in New Mexico. I continued to look for employment with little success. I even drove a delivery truck for six months until my drivers' license was revoked due to the MS. I guessed that was the cause. My attitude took a nose dive. In fact it plunged downward out of sight. My weight went from 130 to 96 pounds. I had a difficult time keeping my bra where it belonged," she said, laughing, "and my butt disappeared."

Carlee was silent for a moment. "This counts for six of my ten lost years. While Eileen, my sister, was on vacation from Mountain Home, she invited me to vacation at her residence. I accepted the offer immediately and moved myself and one suitcase to Idaho.

"The first week I was there, I was ill and hardly went outside. During the second week, I applied for a job at a coffee house. They hired me on the spot." She brightened. "I was so happy, I declared myself a success, and I have not looked back." Carlee lost her smile again. "Except I have been lonely, oh so lonely. When you called me on the phone, I could not believe I was listening to Arthur's voice. I responded immediately and hoped I was not making a fool out of myself. When I asked if you were the real Arthur Haley, you started to play-act and issue an ATC clearance. I knew then that it was you." She took a deep breath and looked kindly at him. "Arthur, it is now up to you to fill me in."

Arthur began by admitting he left the facility early in 1967 but did not leave the Chicago area until late 1968. "The riots that consumed the ghetto part of Chicago and the buses that were turned over and burned in 1968 convinced me to leave. I drove my car from Cicero, where I lived, to St. Louis, Missouri and then, three days later, I left for Los Angeles. Driving west was great as long as I was generally heading toward Denver. However, when I got past Denver, I found my happiness disappearing with every mile. Within a hundred miles, I turned around and went back to Denver, the town I grew up in.

"I have lived in the Denver area since late 1968, however I too had to deal with failure. It was, I thought, considered a failure to be forced out of the best job in the world because of one's inability to pass a Class II physical. I could not convince myself it was okay that I still had a pay check, as that seemed to not matter."

Arthur tried unsuccessfully to reach Carlee through friends and also the personnel department at Des Plaines, Illinois. He became depressed, disillusioned and extremely lonely. He kept looking until one day a friend, still at the Chicago, O'Hare Control Tower, called to ask him a question.

"I asked him if he had your phone number," Arthur told her. "He said yes." Arthur then said. "Carlee, now you are all caught up except for the lost loves of girl-friends and mixed relationships and aspects of my life that embarrass me when I think of participating in such behavior. I will say I did not live up to the life my earthly father or my Heavenly Father deemed appropriate. I will tell you the details if you sincerely want to know. Otherwise, I will skip the horrible part of my life."

Carlee asked, "How many girlfriends did you have?"

"Too many not so good ones." He smiled at her. "Now I have just one, and her name is Carlee. No one else will do." Arthur then said, "I did not ask you how many boyfriends you had because I did not want to know."

She shook her head. "I can be honest with you. Because I lost so much weight, I looked horrible. I was embarrassed. I hope I look better now that I have gained some. At least my bra stays where it belongs."

Arthur said, "I am now a jealous person, and I have a need to know if you ever had a male friend that was important enough to you to enjoy sex."

Carlee looked Arthur in the eye and said, "I am sorry to admit I have never had sex with anyone. Yes, after listening to some of the women at the Control Tower, I thought I would enjoy it, but when I was called dirty names, I tried not to think of it. For a long time, I had a poor image of myself, one no one would want."

Arthur was satisfied with Carlee's story. Arthur made a pot of coffee for himself and poured a glass of ice water for Carlee. He opened a package of cookies, and they enjoyed a snack.

"How long has it been since you've seen your parents?"

Carlee became excited. "Three years."

"Would you like to take a trip to see them?"

She smiled her magic smile. That gave Arthur the answer. He told Carlee he would take her home to see them if she wanted him to. She cried and said, "Yes, how soon?"

Arthur asked, "How soon can you be excused from your job?"

"Immediately!"

"Can we plan a trip to include a stop-over at the Mayo Clinic for a discussion with the medical providers at that facility?"

Carlee agreed. They began to plan.

***

Arthur went to the bank in Mountain Home and showed them his documentation of available money on deposit at the First National Bank of Cicero, Illinois. He withdrew a thousand dollars. Then he and Carlee departed Mountain Home for the Mayo Clinic in Rochester, Minnesota. Carlee was, at first, depressed and in a bad mood. But after a few miles, she and Arthur agreed on one thing—to take this trip with the illusion that everything was going to be okay.

Arthur could tell Carlee was sad to leave her sister. They drove most of the day. Arthur kept thinking of Carlee and her beauty, and he would look across the front seat of his car and want her physically, sexually. He kept driving, but her beauty continued to instill from mother- nature the obvious within a man. To want someone you have loved for years and had to deny yourself the enjoyment of togetherness and to find alternative pleasures, is not good.

They stopped and ate lunch, filled the gas tank, and discussed changing their plans so they could drive to Albuquerque and then to Rochester. This pleased Carlee, and Arthur changed direction. Arthur listened more than talked, but Carlee's brain was working overtime. He encouraged her by periodically commenting that he understood.

"I was desperate to find suitable employment," Carlee said. "A job that would demand performance, provide a challenge, and provide achievement satisfaction. Genuine self-satisfaction. I wanted to accomplish something no one else could do, to provide legal separation between two, three, eight or more aircraft flying at speeds in excess of 180 to 350 knots per hour and walk away from a radar vectoring session and be able to tell myself, I did it."

Arthur continued to drive and listen while Carlee talked. Finally, she went to sleep. She slept for three hours, only turning in the seat once. Almost instantly, she awakened as if startled. She looked around—eyes wide and darting from one thing to the next. She began to mutter, "Where am I? What are we doing? Who are you?"

Arthur was alarmed, but he merely said, calmly, "Carlee, it is Arthur. Arthur Haley. We are going on a vacation in the car."

Carlee began to calm herself and reached over to hug Arthur. He drove the car to the side of the road and stopped. They hugged as Carlee cried for a long time.

Arthur woke to the sound of a pecking noise on the window of his car. He noticed a uniformed officer and rolled the window down.

"Officer. Can I help you?"

"Is everything okay?" the uniformed man asked.

"Yes. We're fine. Just tired."

The Officer looked over at Carlee and then said, "You will need to proceed to a rest stop ahead. You are parked too close to the highway for safety."

Starting his car, Arthur thanked the Officer and then drove down the highway. After a few minutes, he asked Carlee, "Are you hungry?"

"Yes," she said.

Arthur pulled over at the next restaurant, and they ordered dinner. Carlee was silent, but occasionally she would smile at Arthur. He relaxed and said, "Carlee, I love you. Only you. This is not an illusion." He felt life was back to the way it should be.

***

Arthur and Carlee enjoyed visiting her parents and informing them of their plans.

"We will be back after taking care of some important business," Carlee said.

Both Mother and Father received them warmly and wished them the best in life.

Arthur and Carlee arrived at the Mayo Clinic in Rochester, Minnesota. They were welcomed warmly and courteously. Arthur tried to calm Carlee's stress and her feelings of uncertainty and fear. He understood the process and tried to help talk her through it.

"I have been through this stuff many times," Carlee said, "and I know there will be no benefit."

Arthur listened thoughtfully. He wanted to tell her how much he loved her, but decided this was not the time for such comments. He wrote a note to himself to discuss past medical treatments in the hopes that he could better understand what Carlee was coping with. He tucked the note in his pocket for later.

At one point during counseling, the medical consultants excused themselves. "We need to call in additional consultants," they said. "They will be here shortly."

While Carlee and Arthur were waiting, Arthur held her hand and tried to whisper comforting words. When that didn't work, he merely sat close to her and asked her to explain what she perceived was going on. If she could explain her past experience, she might take a more positive approach to the present effort by medical professionals. He hoped they would achieve greater success.

Their physical closeness seemed to help Carlee. She smiled and reached for his hand, holding it firmly.

When the follow-up team arrived, Arthur explained the need to stay close to Carlee, and nobody objected. The new team asked their questions, and Carlee answered without hesitation. After the interview, the couple was informed that a third team would attend to them briefly.

"Do you need or want something to drink such as, coffee, tea, water, milk?"

"Coffee," Arthur said. "And water for Carlee."

The third team of doctors asked many of the same questions. Toward the end of the briefing, one of them said, "We'll provide a written copy of our interviews. After we have studied these over, we'll have another discussion about the next course of action, hopefully before the end of the day." They stood to leave. "This should take only thirty to forty-five minutes. You're welcome to visit the cafeteria while you wait."

Carlee and Arthur stood, but before they could leave, another of the team informed them they would be provided lodging and food for the evening. "We'd like the medical team to have an opportunity to prepare their recommendations. After you've had a chance to digest everything, we'll ask for your decision tomorrow."

Arthur and Carlee left for the cafeteria. It felt good to walk and get some fresh air. They were consumed with the need to know what the professionals were looking for and what they would find.

"We certainly need to work on our patience and our discipline," Carlee said.

For the first time since the couple had reconnected two days earlier, Carlee looked Arthur in the eyes and said, "I love you." Then she hugged him and began to cry.

Arthur held Carlee and thought of their time in Chicago. "Everything is going to be okay," he said. "Jesus told me so." Arthur had a very strong faith in God, but he seldom talked about it. His faith stayed in the background of his life except when it influenced his behavior and drove his conscience to keep him out of trouble. He believed Carlee was a person of great values, but he really did not know of her relationship with God.

After they returned to wait in the clinicians' office, Arthur asked, "Carlee, do you feel comfortable enough to talk with me about your faith in God?"

Carlee looked Arthur in the eyes and said in a very firm manner, "I am always prepared to talk with you about my relationship with God." She lowered her eyes. "I seldom approach this subject because of what occurred at the radar room in Chicago, but I am thrilled to talk with you about it. What do you want to know?"

"Are you a born-again Christian or did you somehow escape that experience?"

Carlee replied, "I went to a Southern Baptist Church until I was thirteen. During this time, I was saved and Baptized. I learned to pray every day until about two years before I left Chicago. I cannot explain why I stopped, but I did." She asked, "Does that answer your question?"

"Thank you, yes. I am pleased."

"Does that mean you are a born-again Christian, too?"

Arthur nodded. "Yes, and I have been for many years."

They hugged each other with joy and happiness.

The medical team captain returned and asked them to accompany her to a conference room where they could discuss the results of their findings and offer Carlee some answers.

***

Carlee and Arthur followed the doctor into the conference room. Carlee half expected to hear the jury deliver a verdict of death, or at least severe debilitation due to her condition that had gone from bad to worse. She feared she would never have a quality of life worth living. The two held hands and silently prayed to Jesus that a miracle be allowed to happen and their lives be given one more chance to survive.

The team leader stood behind a podium and said, "The findings of the Mayo Clinic Medical Team consists of four parts." She looked sympathetically at the couple. "Carlee, you have been diagnosed with Multiple Sclerosis (MS)." She let that sink in for a moment before going on. "After our interviews, we've concluded that an important factor in your health has to do with stress. It's important to manage it if you are going to recover from the attacks that happen from this disease. A healthier lifestyle that includes better nutrition and more stable relationships would certainly improve your responses. We recommend that you attend an institution of your choice to seek counseling. At the current time, it might benefit you to schedule a long and enjoyable vacation with no interruptions." She smiled at Carlee. "The objective of the Mayo Clinic team is to give you recommendations that will help jump-start your treatment. Do you have any questions for us?"

Carlee and Arthur sat in silence, head bowed and tears flowing from their eyes.

After a moment, Arthur said, "Nothing at the moment. We will, to the best of our abilities, begin to make the changes you suggested." He looked at Carlee. "We will need to make some phone calls to our families. Thank you."

Carlee and Arthur left the clinic and walked to the car. They stood outside for a moment. After standing with their arms around each other, they gently kissed each other.

"At least I know now," Carlee said. "I intend to do everything they said I should, starting with calling my sister and my parents."

Arthur handed her his cell phone and said, "Get at it, Carlee."

***

While Carlee was talking with her parents and sister, Arthur drove to an upscale motel and made reservations for the two of them. He also arranged for both of them to receive a therapeutic massage after dinner, accompanied by their choice of wine while listening to their favorite music. When they arrived at the hotel, a representative presented Carlee with a dozen red roses.

Carlee gave Arthur a kiss followed by a long hug.

"I know the news has been bad, but I feel like our love is even stronger," Arthur said, noting that Carlee's smile was the most beautiful he'd ever seen. After they had checked into their room, the two enjoyed a wonderful massage and a relaxing glass of wine. Arthur could see that Carlee's stress was easing. They had taken the first step of many as directed by the clinic, and they intended to take all the remaining steps in due time.

That evening, as Arthur lay next to Carlee, he found it difficult to breath. He was having flashbacks to his time in Chicago, and he did not want to concern her with his sordid recollections and memories. Arthur wanted only to concentrate on a future with Carlee. He managed to recover his confidence as he held Carlee and kissed her time and time again, periodically wiping tears from her eyes.

"This is our time," he said. "Lets you and I enjoy it."

As they looked into each other's eyes, they simultaneously began to sing *Why Me Lord*.

When Carlee nodded, Arthur knew it was okay.

"It's the Lord's will," Carlee said. "A long time ago, I walked to the personnel office in Chicago and asked for your phone number. They said they did not have a forwarding number for you. I walked out of the office, crying." Her eyes teared up at the memory. "I was alone. I have been alone for ten years. Tonight, all that seems a bad dream, and one I want to forget."

"Tonight I want you," Arthur told her. "To hold each other and thank our Heavenly Father for bringing us back together today. I am having a difficult time believing it is true."

Carlee pinched Arthur on the neck and said, "I believe you must be Arthur Haley, and I am Carlee Jenkins, and we are holding each other. Now I am going to kiss you again and again."

They committed themselves to each other and made love for the first time.

***

In the morning, Arthur awakened to the need for a cup of hot black coffee and wanted time to think about their next step. The events of yesterday had healed deep-seated feelings of loneliness and gave impetus to a positive future for two people who had longed for each other during the cold and windy Chicago nights. Looking at Carlee now smiling and happy as he lay next to her, Arthur began to believe in miracles.

"We can beat this," he said when she opened her eyes.

She wanted to agree.

They both thought of the miracle of life and wondered if they had possibly gotten pregnant during their love-making the night before. They held each other again, wanting to be reassured they were alive and not dreaming.

Later, they ordered room service. While they ate, they planned their next travel schedule beginning in three days.

Arthur thought, "What a life. Bring it on."

***

Arthur and Carlee realized that their future would be uncertain and difficult to envision as her Multiple Sclerosis could impact her health every day, even in subtle ways. They began to research the most reputable and effective counseling and therapeutic institution available to them and would seek their assistance as soon as they found the right organization. MS could be a devastating disease, and one that could cause the central nervous system to send signals that complicate any diagnosis. Sometimes an incorrect diagnosis could result in care plans improperly implemented and valuable time wasted.

As they began to plan their wedding, Carlee became the major influence in Arthur's life—where they would live and how to proceed knowing they had to cope with MS. A big concern was how to make a living knowing that any day could be Carlee's last. They both had a medical retirement, medical insurance and a future to be determined, but this was more than either of them had contemplated for years. They were determined to make the best of their situation, and they were going to love each other every moment of every day.

The previous ten years had taken its toll on both of them—years of depression, deep and lasting hurt. Somehow, they had come to grips with this reality. They knew they must get these horrible years behind them, including the experiences they had yet to share with each other.

Separately, they started lists of those things that they had tried to suppress. It was difficult, but they persisted, trying not to leave out important happenings in their lives. They were determined to overcome their frustrations and fears, to cling to each other and be resolute in determining the best course of action for the two of them. Not separately or alone, but together.

After reviewing numerous services, making several phone calls and listening to their options, Arthur and Carlee decided to investigate two options. If they didn't like the first option, they could change to the other organization.

On their first meeting, they were asked to brief the counselor on their backgrounds.

"I completed two years of college in Albuquerque, New Mexico in 1959," Carlee said. "When I noticed an advertisement for air traffic controllers in a magazine, I applied for a position in the terminal part of the program and was accepted. I completed the technical training in Oklahoma City. Then I was assigned to the facility known as the Terminal Radar Approach Control or (TRACON) facility in Chicago. I was excited and studied har to get certified on the tower functions and two radar positions.

"I was diagnosed with Multiple Sclerosis, but I tried to deal with it and continue the certification process. One day while training on a radar arrival position, my training instructor became upset at the lack of progress I was making and yelled at me. He called me a dirty name."

"What did he call you?" the counselor asked.

Carlee looked shy. "He called me a cunt. Since most of the employees were male, this really embarrassed me. The men whooped and hollered and started repeating the word. I stood and told my instructor I was leaving."

"And did you?"

"Yes. I left the room and went to look for my friend Arthur." She glanced in his direction. "I could not find him, and when I asked someone from the administrative office if they knew where he was, they said Arthur had left the organization about a month before. I was sickened when I heard."

Arthur reached over and squeezed her hand.

"When I discussed my situation, I learned I was being terminated due to a low or unsatisfactory performance. The next day while in the training room, I was informed I had been medically disqualified due to MS and would not be allowed to complete my certification to become a Full Performance Level Controller. I asked for sick leave as I could not think straight, and I wanted to locate Arthur. Ever since arriving at the facility, he had always helped me. We had become good friends. Now that he was gone, I did not know what to do. I took three days off and consulted my private physician. He was the one who confirmed I had MS.

"My doctor was familiar with FAA policies regarding Class II Physicals. I asked if my disease would prevent me from working in the FAA. He said it would take a miracle for me to be permitted to work live air traffic again and suggested I look elsewhere for a career."

This time, Carlee wiped away tears. "I fought that decision for months and lost. Eventually, I applied for medical disability retirement, and it was approved."

"I wish I had known," Arthur interjected. "I might have been more help to you."

Carlee shook her head. "You couldn't have done anything. I left the facility and tried to make a go of it on my own without a job. My health deteriorated, and I entered a hospital where I stayed for two years and a few months. When hospital personnel started talking about releasing me, I almost panicked. One of the nurses who had helped take care of me said I could live with her. Jackie was her name. She had wanted to move into a different apartment, so we agreed to share the cost, and I left the hospital.

"Everything was working fine until she allowed her boyfriend to move in. I tolerated him and his inappropriate advances towards me for six months, but then I asked Jackie if he could leave. Jackie asked why. When I told her he was attempting to have sex with me, she kicked him out. Things were good again for about a year. But she found another boyfriend, and the same situation started up again. This time, Jackie became upset with me! She called me a prude and said I'd never had sex with anyone. I told her that was none of her business, and then *she* tried to have sex with me."

This time, Arthur looked angry. "I'm sorry that happened to you," he said.

"The saddest thing is, I had avoided having sex outside of a married relationship for so long—and suffered so many vindictive remarks from other women—that I actually considered starting a Lesbian relationship with Jackie." She gave an uneasy laugh.

Everyone was quiet, waiting for Carlee to continue.

"But this was more than I could accept. I helped Jackie locate another apartment. On the day I tried to move into my own smaller apartment, my doctor put me in the hospital again. I broke the lease, lost my security deposit and had my belongings stored. I did not know what else to do."

Arthur put his arm around Carlee until she could compose herself.

"During this stay in the hospital, I lost so much weight I hardly recognized myself. During nights, when I tried to sleep, I would wake up with weird thoughts. When I began asking strange questions of the nurses, they moved me to a mental wing of the hospital. I stayed for nine or ten months.

"I continued to lose weight all the way down to 67 pounds. I'm five feet eight inches tall and had weighed 130 pounds when I worked at the ATC facility. After losing all this weight, I looked horrible. Even my fingers were skinny and ugly. My clothes did not fit.

"My dad drove all the way from Albuquerque to Chicago to see me. He took one look at me and said, 'Honey, you are going home with me, so start thinking how we are going to get this done.' I had lost my ability to walk, and the hospital staff refused to release me."

Carlee smiled a little at the memory. "Dad told the hospital staff it did not matter, he was taking me home. Initially I was happy, but after an hour or so in the car, I began to feel ill and fainted. My father saw a Highway Patrol Officer and asked him for assistance. The officer directed us to a clinic where the doctors said I could not travel. We checked into a motel close by. The next day I went back to the clinic. The doctor told my father I was too ill to travel, and he admitted me to the hospital. My father informed me he was going home, and he left."

At this point, both the counselor and Arthur looked shocked.

"He just left you there?" Arthur asked.

She nodded her head. "I wondered what I was going to do next. I was scared and confused. It was a terrible time. I was stranded at the hospital in St. Louis and did not know anyone. I became desperate to meet and become friendly with one of the nurses. I seemed to have better luck with the LPN's as they were friendly. Finally, after several months one of them asked me what I was going to do. I told them I would find an apartment and say good bye to this hospital. All I do is lose weight. She offered almost the same deal as my previous roommate in Chicago, but I was better prepared for this one.

"No boyfriends moving in and causing trouble, I told her. Luckily, it worked well for two years. I improved somewhat but nothing to brag about. I purchased a computer and began to research my medical condition. I learned a lot, and some of what I learned depressed me, but I kept reading. I finally found a diet that was for MS patients. I participated every day and started feeling better. I gained weight. I got a job to keep my mind off of myself and to help pay expenses.

"The hospital told me I owed them over $30,000.00. I showed them my health benefit information and told them to collect it from the insurance as I was otherwise broke. I kept my job which was totally inadequate from a salary perspective, but I eventually got a promotion. I tried to call my parents, but I always seemed to get the wrong number. And because my father had left me in St. Louis,

I did not try very hard to get it right. I was really upset with him and my mother. I thought they could have done more. Eventually, I sent them a package for Christmas, and they responded. We talked a couple of times, and Mother asked me to move in with them. I decided to do that.

"I took the bus and then rented a car to drive to my own car. It had been parked in the driveway of the apartment for over two years, and with an expired license plate and no insurance. I thought to myself, what else can go wrong. The cabbie jumped my battery and the car started. I drove it to a filling station, filled it with gas, checked the oil and windshield washer fluid, and drove to Albuquerque. I got sick three times while driving, but I kept saying to myself, do not stop. Once, the car sputtered, and I noticed the fuel gauge was on empty. I ran across a filling station within one block. Lucky me. One time I began to get dizzy and confused and stopped for food. That was all I needed until I got home. My mother cried herself to sleep the night I arrived.

***

"Mother was great—loving and caring. My father, however, seemed distant and did not understand why I was fatigued and felt bad most of the time. We had always had a loving relationship. Soon I concluded that he did not know what to do to help. That frustrated and confused him, and caused him to avoid me which only added stress to my life. I spent most of my time in my room or in the backyard, and tried to limit time with my father. It did reduce conflict between us, but I always felt uncomfortable around him.

"My sister sent me letters telling me about Idaho, and soon I thought about going there. She came to visit and asked if I would like to live with her for a while. I asked if I should plan for a longer stay or just a vacation. I needed to know as I was too weak to relocate. She suggested I try it for a month. If things improved for me, we'd play it a day at a time.

"Mother and I both cried when I left. My father was very stoic even though he was worried about me, but he supported the idea me living with my sister. On the way to Mountain Home, Idaho, I initially was very sad to leave Mother. I had dreamed of getting well and possibly being a mother myself. That brought back the accusation the nurse had made about me never having sex. I began to worry that I was abnormal and might never want sex.

"Then, when I looked in the mirror and saw my body without boobs, it was easy to become depressed over and over.

"My stay in Mountain Home was very good for me. I was happier with my sister than at any time before, except when I was working at O'Hare Tower in Chicago. I gained about thirty pounds and started feeling more energetic. I was able to get a job performing menial tasks.

"During the last six months, I began living again. When I received a phone call from Arthur, I became so excited. I could hardly contain my enthusiasm, and my imagination went wild. I had memories that almost did not seem real. When he showed up, I almost fainted. Arthur was someone who I thought I would never see again. I had lost hope. When I held him, I knew life had just taken a turn for the better. I actually prayed again—something I had completely forgotten to do for years. Now I realize just how much I was messed up. I know I must have forgotten some of the difficult times, but I am so happy today. That is all I can think of. Thank you for letting me talk."

When Carlee was silent for a while, Arthur bowed his head. "I wish I had left contact information for you when I left O'Hare. Maybe your health wouldn't have suffered so much."

The counselor smiled at them both. "It seems that you two are committed to each other. It will be a lot of work, Arthur, but you have certainly done Carlee a lot of good."

"I really want to provide a good life for us from here on out."

"Then perhaps you should share your own experiences over these last few years."

Arthur was hesitant at first, but then he decided to open up. "Prior to 1956, I was an Air Traffic Control Specialist at the Chicago O'Hare tower. I had recently been promoted to a First Line Supervisor, normally called Team Supervisor, and I was thrilled. Needless to say, when I lost my medical and was disqualified for the position, I was horribly upset. I had failed to pass my Class II Physical and could no longer control live air traffic. I applied for medical retirement, and it was approved. But I was an emotional wreck and refused to talk with anyone. When I left the facility, I did not leave any forwarding information.

"Later, when I was attempting to contact Carlee, they said she had failed the training program, too. They told me she had resigned. I began to have serious disagreements with my girlfriend and ultimately, we split.

"I stayed in Illinois but became disillusioned with everything I tried to do. I would walk the streets of Des Plaines, wondering to where the NTSB previously held the hearings on the DL 42 and NC 10 accident. Nothing seemed to make sense to me.

"I took numerous menial jobs only to get severely upset at fellow workers as I could not achieve job satisfaction and ultimately resigned—each time burning the bridge I just crossed. I told myself I did not need the work, the money, or the people. I ended up drinking alcohol by the bottle, then by the quart. I knew I was wasting away as I lost weight from my normal 190 pounds down to 110.

"I sought professional help from a female counselor who was of a mixed Hispanic and French heritage. She was beautiful. We started dating—I'm sure she was not supposed to date her patients—and I ended up causing her to start drinking. We almost got married, but she fell in love with someone other than me. An attorney with a lot of money. I lost all respect for both lawyers and counselors.

"I wasted several years of my life going from one menial job to another and from one relationship to another until I found myself in a closed bar in Atlanta, Georgia, not sure how I got there. I bought an airline ticket back to Chicago Midway, but in the parking lot, I could not find my car. Several days later, I remembered that I's driven it to Atlanta. I flew back to get it, but when I tried to leave the parking lot, the attendant could not calculate the amount of money I owed him. It had been more than three months, and the ticket had expired. He was new on the job and did not want to make a mistake. I asked him what would happen if the ticket was destroyed and nothing collected? He tore it up, and I left. If I had been honest, I should have paid over $200.00.

"That winter in Chicago, I spent three different periods of time in rehab. Every job I got, which were many, I quit or had difficulties with fellow workers and supervisors and got fired. During my time away from the job, I walked the floor of my apartment and the streets of Des Plaines. I started to drink again and tried on my own to quit. I got another job and then a second one. I was working sixteen to eighteen hours a day, six days a week. On my one day off, I walked the river bank, keeping busy so I would not want to return to alcohol. I even tried fishing in a river I knew had no fish. One day, after years of that life, I decided to change.

"When I was young, I recall my father telling me to always trust in God. To always practice my faith in Jesus Christ and to believe. Believe in God and miracles. I visited a local Catholic Church, then a Lutheran Church. During the week, I would watch religious services on TV.

"I heard Joel Osteen and made it a practice to listen to him each time I got a chance. His message of faith and hope was encouraging to me. I drove to my father's grave site in Oklahoma and prayed. My father had divorced my mother many years ago, and I was ashamed that I didn't even know if she was alive or dead.

"On my way back to Chicago, I called a friend of mine who I had once worked with. When he didn't answer, looked up the phone number for the control tower and dialed it. My friend answered the phone. We caught up on past times. I asked him if he had ever heard of Carlee Jenkins, and he said yes. He and the guys had been talking about her the previous week. One of the guys remembered seeing her in the hospital when he'd visited his sister there. He got her phone number. Through a series of phone calls, I tracked Carlee to Mountain Home, Idaho.

"When Carlee answered the phone, I immediately thought my father was right. God performs miracles."

He looked over at Carlee who was crying.

***

Arthur wondered what Carlee was thinking of him and whether his story would increase her anxiety. He hoped the counselor would jump in with something that would save him. When that didn't happen, he asked, "Can you outline the steps you think we need to take?"

The counselor was no longer smiling. "I would suggest that the two of you set up separate counseling sessions twice a week, and joint counseling once a week. Heeling will require time and commitment." She flipped open a folder and took some notes. "When I am dealing with Carlee's issues, it may benefit you both if Arthur sat in eventually." She looked at Carlee. "He is an integral player in your recovery. He can help you recognize important steps and practice them when I am not present." She turned to Arthur. "Not that I want you to do anything except to avoid complicating matters."

When the couple nodded understanding, the counselor added, "Both of you need to focus on several basic factors that can help in the immediate future. To start with, Carlee's diet needs to follow a strict practice of proper nutrition along with the drinking of plenty of liquids, mainly water and fruit juices. No sodas, coffee, tea, etc. I will provide each of you with a recommended diet within a week.

"The second focus will be the development of a realistic exercise program designed to increase muscle development and strength, and simultaneously improve body functions. Please do not take this part for granted. It takes commitment and hard work to improve the body and internal systems so they will perform their assigned functions. This should also improve emotional health and return your zest for life, including for sex.

"The third focus we will undertake will be the medical treatment in order that you can recover from your most recent attack and manage the progression of the disease."

She turned again to Arthur. "You will play a significant role by reinforcing the treatment advocated by her physician, therefore you must understand each process and ask questions of the doctor if you do not."

He nodded agreement.

"Carlee, I will be in contact with your physician and will discuss his qualifications and the necessary care strategies. Since you are the patient, I want you to monitor and evaluate the benefit or lack thereof from this treatment. That is of the greatest importance."

The counselor leaned back in her chair. "We have had success in our previous patients, and we intend to see a significant benefit and improvement in your case as well." She stood to indicate that their meeting was coming to an end. "This covers the three steps I plan to take in dealing with your issues. I will assess progress we make over the next few weeks. Meanwhile, try to stay positive. Attitude is crucial."

She stepped from behind her desk and walked up to Carlee, taking her hand. "I am confident your health will improve. It's up to you and Arthur to reduce unnecessary stress in your daily life. Remember, life is good." She shook Arthur's hand before escorting the couple to the door. "Check with my assistant to schedule the next three sessions with both of you." She bid them goodbye.

They walked to their car and were as giddy as two people could be. Everything seemed to be funny, and they both laughed whether it was humorous or not. They held hands as though they were two high-school kids skipping school.

They stopped at a small café.

"How long do you think the counselor will want us to stay in the area before we could move elsewhere?" Carlee asked.

"Maybe it's up to us. Do you have any preferences?"

Carlee's eyes widened. "You mean I might have a choice?"

Arthur nodded and said, "Yes."

It did not take long for Carlee to decide. "Albuquerque. I would like to be near my mother. She is such a sweetheart."

"We must move to Albuquerque, then," Arthur said, looking into Carlee's eyes—those eyes that always melted his heart. "I think we should talk about the second focus mentioned by the counselor. Carlee, will you promise me one very important thing?"

"Sure, what is it?"

"I am going to really get into this recovery process, and I know me. I can become excessively focused. I do not want to overdo or push too hard. I want you to be candid and honest."

She nodded.

"I'm serious. Once we get started, I may not be able to determine how much to push and when to stop. You, my love, will need to tell me when to slow down or stop."

Carlee, with a grin on her face asked, "Does that also apply when we are making love to each other?"

Arthur could tell Carlee was already in a better mood, and he was pleased.

She reached for his hand and squeezed it. "I promise to tell you, but I intend to work hard and get stronger. This weakened state of my health tends to depress me, and I am encouraged that someone who knows what they are doing is looking out for my best interest."

They pulled a brochure from their treasure of documents given to them by the counselor and identified the one on exercise.

After reading the first paragraph, Carlee looked at Arthur and laughed. "Honey, I am already tired," she said.

Arthur appreciated her sense of humor. He looked out the window of the cafe and said, "I'm not letting you back in the car until we've had a four mile hike."

They both broke into laughter.

They decided to return to their apartment and begin some serious thinking about their future. On the way, Arthur asked,

"Did you really mean it when you mentioned Albuquerque as a place to live?"

Carlee simply said, "Yes."

When they arrived home, Arthur retrieved the apartment lease and checked the date. It expired in three months.

"Do you really think it's possible to return to my hometown?"

"How long have you been gone?"

Carlee started to tear up. "It's been over ten years. My mother would be so happy."

Arthur held her and said, " Carlee, you and I can make it happen. Do you want to?"

She cried like a baby, and that gave Arthur her answer.

After a few moments, he said, "We should discuss this with the counselor so we can keep our commitment to your health. I firmly believe this is consistent with the Mayo Clinic Team recommendation to do whatever is necessary to reduce stress."

Carlee agreed. They hugged each other and thanked God for a miracle.

***

Arthur and Carlee went to bed early that night, but laid there with eyes wide open and their brains pacing from thought to thought, idea to idea. They held each other and prayed, thanking their Lord and Savior.

Arthur awoke early the next morning, made coffee and walked around the block. When he returned, Carlee was taking a shower and singing. Arthur thought it was the most beautiful song he ever heard and he told her so.

"What do you want for breakfast?" he asked through the shower curtain.

Over the sound of sunning water, Carlee said, "I looked in the diet book and checked the refrigerator; but drew a blank."

"Maybe we go to the restaurant for a diet-friendly meal followed by a trip to the grocery store."

Breakfast was delicious. Arthur thought the coffee tasted especially good.

As Carlee sipped on her juice, she said, "I never did like coffee, so please don't sweat drinking it in front of me. I'm not tempted."

They made a grocery list and, for the first time since they got back together, Carlee mentioned her finances. "I must call my bank. I think I am low on cash."

"I have money, and you are free to use it," Arthur told her.

She gave him a sideways grin. "Honey, how soon can we get married so we can merge our bank accounts?" Facetiously, she said, "I think ex-supervisors made more money than ex- trainee's. Your retirement should be more than mine."

Arthur quickly said, "Sweetheart, what is mine is yours, and what is yours is mine, and don't you forget it."

Not to be outdone, Carlee said as quickly, "We must hurry home so I can take advantage of you for a long time, and then again and again."

Arthur smiled knowing this was a win. They hurried home, forgetting about which grocery store they preferred."

As they joined each other in bed, Arthur noticed again her beautiful eyes and fabulous smile. "This is one Arthur who is committed to your improved health," he thought. He remembered the horrible experiences she endured while spending all that time in hospitals and worrying about where to live and how to live when released. For a moment, he became emotional and needed time to collect himself.

Carlee brought him back to the present when she threw off the sheet and offered herself to him.

***

Early the next morning, they awoke with the urge to express themselves again. Arthur tried to restrain himself, only to yield to the joy of Carlee. Afterward, they lay close to each other and talked about Mountain Home and Carlee's time with her sister. This had been a great time for Carlee—a job she had to occupy her time, the freedom to walk and dream, and a life without the hassle of a roommate who obviously did not understand the complexities of her health diagnosis.

When Arthur mentioned Carlee's father, she got quiet and then wanted to move on.

"My father and I had a wonderful relationship," Arthur said, "before he passed. More like the one you have with your mother."

"She and I were close. We shared many beautiful moments, even if it was just over the phone." She talked more about the time with her sister.

Suddenly, Arthur said, "Loving you is not enough. I want you to experience God's goodness."

***

The apartment they were living in was located east of the airport directly in line with one of the runways at O'Hare. Arthur had chosen it because of the reduced cost each month. One night, around 11:00

p.m., a large, almost unbearable noise shook them out of their bed. In a panic, vacated their apartment. Windows in most of the buildings were broken, and people emptied into the streets. Within seconds, they heard a loud noise at the airport and anticipated the worst. They learned later that a Cessna Citation departing one runway had hit a B-727 making a sharp right turn to land on another. The B727 pilot experienced difficulty keeping it airborne as it passed over their apartment. As the pilot maneuvered the larger plane in for landing, he managed to make it to the runway but crash landed the aircraft approximately 6,000 feet past the normal touchdown point. Arthur and Carlee were relieved to learn that all of passengers were able to deplane and walk away from the accident.

The couple began preparing for their second visit to the counselor. They reviewed Carlee's diet and exercise regimen, and the care provided by Carlee's physician.

"Are you prepared to tell her everything, or are there parts you're not going to mention?"

"I am going to be an open book," she said. "I may be embarrassed, but I want to get it out. If we need to deal with some of it, so be it."

"That's what the counselor is there for," Arthur said. "Do you want me to do the same? There was some pretty raunchy stuff in my ten-year history. Some real embarrassing activities that I am not proud of now and wasn't then."

Carlee replied, "We should deal with it, so tell it like it is."

Arthur reluctantly agreed.

They met with the counselor and began by giving a status report on the steps they had taken to comply with her assignment. They inquired if they would be permitted to relocate to Albuquerque and continue with the Mayo team until they got situated in their new home.

"We have offices in Albuquerque," the counselor said. "And besides, you should seek another service, other than me, for the long term. This can be done anywhere, so long as you meet the objectives of the Mayo Clinic. You will need to pick a physician from the list provided by the clinic."

Then the Counselor asked, "When are you planning to relocate?"

Carlee and Arthur said, simultaneously, "Within three months and cancellation of our lease."

"I see no problem with this plan."

Arthur and Carlee began to dream, and Carlee began to wear a permanent smile. They made lists of the things they needed to take care of, having lived in the area periodically, for more than ten years. At their next meeting, the counselor provided names and contact information for Mayo Clinic personnel in Albuquerque. They were free to transfer whenever they thought necessary. Arthur and Carlee departed her office in a state of glee.

They could hardly believe God was continuing to guide them, but they were not complaining. They planned to relocate as soon as Carlee could negotiate an end to her own lease.

At the Garden Grove restaurant that specialized in Polish dishes, they relaxed into the idea that they were already saying good-bye to the Chicago area. As they prepared to leave, Carlee said, "We probably should come here a couple of times before we move."

Jokingly, Arthur said, "Leave. Where are we going?"

Carlee laughed and then sobered. "Nowhere if I don't get out of my lease."

Three months would be difficult to handle as cold weather approached, and Arthur wanted to get on the road before the ice and wind began to fly around the city streets. He contacted Carlee's apartment representative and asked to talk with her in person.

When they met, Arthur explained their situation and told her about Carlee's health issues. "Is it possible she could be released from her lease before the original expiration?"

The representative said, "Arthur, you are a lucky person. We have someone who wants to move in within three weeks and is prepared to sign a lease for two years. If you can pay me the rent due for the next two weeks, or agree that I reimburse you for one half of your deposit, you can vacate any time."

Arthur was crazy with happiness. He hurried to his apartment and informed Carlee to start packing immediately. They called their counselor to inform her of the change in their plans, and she agreed to allow them to come in the next day for guidance. She would have the forwarding recommendation to Albuquerque sent by fax in preparation for their arrival.

Carlee called her mother.

"Really? Oh, sweetheart, I can't wait. I want it to happen today!"

"Soon," she told her mother.

When she hung up the phone, she asked Arthur if they had the money to pay for the rent.

Arthur reminded Carlee they had half of a deposit coming back to them. He considered his bank account, savings account and then, for a moment, he thought about visiting the O'Hare Control Tower. He changed his mind when he remembered what management had done to him. Arthur crossed off his planned visit.

Later, he and Carlee sat in the living room and discussed leaving Chicago.

"I need to close all of my accounts and transfer the funds to Albuquerque. I should also have my car checked over so we can travel as early as possible."

"Yes!" Carlee yelled. "Right this moment."

***

Everything was packed. They left the keys to the apartment with the night watchman. The couple started traveling with everything they owned packed in a four-wheel trailer hooked to Arthur's car. As he pulled out of the driveway, Arthur became nostalgic. Then he remembered that he was leaving with a nice income, the love of his life and a future he had to determine. He was committed to carving out of the best world he could for he and Carlee. They had committed themselves to each other—aware of the obstacles that lay in their paths—and they were optimistic of the future.

Late that afternoon, Arthur sensed Carlee was becoming fatigued. She would try to sleep—napping a restless nap—and then wake up wanting to know where they were.

"Let's stop for the night at Springfield, Missouri," Arthur said.

Carlee put on a bright smile. "I can make it farther if you still feel like driving."

"I appreciate your enthusiasm, but we've had a great day. I need the rest."

They stopped at a nice motel and had food delivered to the room. They watched a Chicago Bears pre-season football game against the St. Louis Cardinals. Within thirty minutes of eating, Carlee was sound asleep.

They left St. Louis around 9:30 the next morning.

"You certainly got your beauty sleep last night," Arthur told her. "If you're not certain, just look in the mirror."

They continued to travel leisurely to ensure Carlee was rested and eating properly. They would stop occasionally for a short walk and a few stretching exercises suggested by the counselor. By mid-afternoon on the fourth day, they reached Albuquerque and made their way to Carlee's parent's home. Arthur was eager to locate an apartment, sign a lease and start living.

Carlee's father asked, "Are you two married?"

"Not yet," she replied. "We will be as soon as we talk to a minister and choose a date. We wanted to be near family so you could attend. It will probably happen this week if everything works out as planned."

Arthur was listening and supporting everything she said.

"I would also like Eileen to participate if she could."

Carlee's mother suggested they call Eileen right away. When they called, her sister said she would love to come if Arthur could wait that long.

"I will call the airlines immediately and let you know when I can be present."

Fifteen minutes later, Eileen let them know she could arrive in Albuquerque by 4:00 p.m. on Thursday and would like to stay for a week. If the wedding could be scheduled within that time frame, she would do whatever Carlee asked of her.

Carlee asked her mother what church she attended.

"The First United Methodist Church of Lexington, New Mexico. It's only three miles from our house."

Carlee asked, "Is that okay with you, Arthur?"

"Definitely," he said.

Carlee got the information from her mother and made the call. They talked for a while and then scheduled the wedding for 4:00 p.m. on Friday.

"Oh, Carlee! I'm so happy," her mother said, hugging her. She pulled back and asked, "Are you going to spend the night with us?"

After dinner, Carlee and Arthur left for a motel for the night. When her Mother asked if she wanted to spend the night at home, Carlee replied, not tonight, perhaps later."

They departed, checked into a motel and enjoyed each other as if they were married. At one point, Carlee suggested something that she had heard the women at the control tower discuss—something out of the ordinary.

Arthur said, "Go for it!"

***

Arthur awakened early and craved a big cup of black coffee. As usual, he wanted time to collect his thoughts in private and to plan for the next few days. He reflected on his past, struggling with leaving a place where he had experienced significant emotional torment while also enjoying great economic and employment achievement. On this morning, he was trying to cope with the thoughts of the past—concerned that he might need to surface the most negative elements of human behavior that one could imagine, much less participate in, as he had done. How could he reveal his past behavior without causing unnecessary or potentially damaging stress for the most important person in his life?

His conscience was not cooperating, and he felt sad. He decided that, if this subject surfaced as necessary to discuss openly, he would set aside a time where he could inform the counselor before he and Carlee had to deal with it. The counselor could help him figure out how to inform Carlee. Arthur knew his past behavior was unbelievably abhorrent and totally unacceptable. He had had a mindset similar to an animal in season—absent of moral convictions and intent on achieving sexual self-satisfaction even at the cost of damage to a woman who had consented to participate in such behavior.

He urgently wanted to cleanse his soul. His conscience was telling him to come clean, to reveal his behavior as directed by the counselor. He wanted to deal with his past behavior, but he did not want Carlee to be forced to acknowledge that he had done such an unacceptable act. This scared Arthur and, when he thought of it, he would dive into a deep sweat. Arthur was on his third cup of coffee when he decided he had to tell the counselor.

It was close to 9:00 a.m.—time to wake Carlee if they were going to meet their appointments. He was tempted to crawl in bed with her, be close to her blue eyes, touch her warm body, look at her beautiful smile. It would have been easy to postpone the agenda for the day, but then he thought, "Discipline Arthur, discipline."

He awakened Carlee, walked out of her bedroom, and said to himself, "Stay calm and think about it later in the day."

During breakfast, Arthur noticed a few colorful autumn leaves had fallen from the trees that bordered the restaurant.

"Are you planning to purchase a wedding dress soon?"

She smiled at Arthur and asked, "What color would you prefer?"

As a novice wedding planner, Arthur said, "I think you should choose something that suits your complexion, but I have no expertise in such matters."

She smiled and said, "How about light blue?"

"That sounds lovely."

"What color suit are you going to wear?"

Arthur thought for a moment. "I will need to buy. I haven't needed a suit for over ten years. I was thinking of a navy blue. How does that sound to you?"

Carlee smiled and said, "I love it. I will decide the color of my dress."

Arthur asked, "Are you going to tell me the color you chose?"

"You will find that out on our wedding day," she said, teasing him.

They began to discuss their agenda for the day—confirm with the minister, set the date, purchase a wedding dress and suit, and have the suit tailored, buy shoes, look for an apartment or house, go to the bank and open an account, transfer savings, decide who will stand up with the groom, find a physician with expertise in MS, and several other must-do-today priorities. Arthur handed the list to Carlee and asked her to review it. When Carlee looked it over, she smiled that beautiful smile, and Arthur knew he had made the right decision. They left the restaurant to begin a busy day.

Arthur recognized Carlee's attention to detail in almost everything, but she was trying to be all things to all people, and her fatigue level was increasing significantly.

"Why don't you go back to the motel and get some rest," he suggested.

She looked at Arthur and asked, "Why?"

"I promised both you and the Mayo Clinic that I would monitor your get up and go. I have detected a drop in your energy level. Therefore, I am suggesting you avoid exerting yourself when it is not wise to do so."

Carlee reluctantly agreed, and they returned to the motel. After making her comfortable and putting out the "Do not disturb" sign, Arthur informed her he was going to run a couple of errands.

While driving around the neighborhood, he saw four houses advertised for sale by the same agent. He copied the phone number and called. When a lady answered, Arthur informed her he was interested in renting or purchasing a house in the area.

"I'm curious, though. Why are so many on the market at one time? Is there a problem with this area?"

The agent chuckled and then said, "A local firm is transferring their employees to another location. Several of the individuals who worked at that firm live in that area." She paused and then said, "I've listed these four, but there are seven others I've listed in another location. None of the owners are interested in renting at this time." She volunteered to set up a showing.

Arthur asked to see the four, as they were in the area he preferred.

"I have a break in my schedule. I can meet you there in thirty minutes, if you'd like."

When they met at the first home, Arthur learned that the houses were all priced in the neighborhood of $165,000.

After looking through the four properties, the agent informed Arthur that possession of the last home could occur upon closing, as the owners were already in the process of moving.

"We're new to town," Arthur said, "but I'm certainly interested in one of these houses."

"Are you prepared to purchase now, or must you wait a while?"

Arthur thought it over. "I'd like to make an offer now, but I'm not sure which is our best option."

The agent volunteered that one of the owners had already purchased a home at their new location and was motivated to sell.

"How motivated?"

"I can't say, but it wouldn't hurt to come in under asking price."

"Point me to a good lending institution, and let's make an offer of $150,000," Arthur told her. "Contingent on my getting a loan for eighty percent of the purchase price."

"I'll have a contract prepared by 5:00 p.m. this evening," she said.

On the way to the motel, Arthur considered the date of the wedding just days away. He decided to wait on contacting the loan officer, as he wanted to apply for the loan and purchase the new home as a married man. He hoped Carlee would approve of the house he chose.

Arriving at the motel, Arthur found Carlee sound asleep. He did not disturb her, but made several phone calls taking care of many of the priorities they had discussed. He went to a men's clothing store and purchased his suit and asked for it be tailored within two days. The salesman agreed to meet that date.

When Arthur returned to the motel Carlee was up, feeling great and wanting to get things done. Jokingly, she got a piece of paper and said, "I am going to practice." Then she wrote, "Mrs. Carlee Arthur's Wife."

Carlee laughed at her own joke. Arthur smiled because he knew she was happy.

***

Eileen and her husband arrived early on Thursday and set to work helping with the wedding plans. The wedding party met with the minister who informed them that the church chapel was available, and all was good.

Arthur turned to Eileen's husband and said, "I hope you would do me the honor of being my best man for this occasion." He agreed.

The wedding on Friday was beautiful, but not as beautiful as Carlee. Everyone ate a delicious meal following the ceremony. Even Carlee's father seemed to enjoy himself. All through the evening, Carlee and Arthur hugged and kissed, touching each other to prove to themselves that each was real. Thinking of their past and then living their current experience was almost unimaginable.

Eight days after arriving in Albuquerque, Carlee and Arthur were husband and wife, and living in their own home. They did not have a lot of furniture, but that didn't seem to matter. They stood in the middle of the living room, vacant as it was, and gave a prayer of thanksgiving to their Lord and Savior Jesus Christ.

***

Waking up in their home with only the essentials of furniture around them, Carlee and Arthur rejoiced, hugged each other, laughed and cried. Unable to contain their feelings, their emotions were dancing all over. They expressed themselves openly and candidly, almost as if they were in another world. Over the next few days, they invited everyone to stop by as they had not had, prior to that moment, the opportunity for family to visit in their home.

They asked, "God, is this really true? Do we have our own home?"

A call came from the Mayo Clinic counseling service requesting they make an appointment for the following day to resume therapy. Carlee and Arthur discussed their schedule and then agreed to an appointment at 10:00 a.m. the next day. They would be meeting with a Dr. Brookfield. She gave them an assignment for the meeting.

"Please give this assignment plenty of thought," Dr. Brookfield said, "as I want both of you to be prepared to reveal every possible detail of your life experiences to each other when we meet. As your counselor, I need to know your background, and this is the most effective way. Additionally, this will help you become aware of the other persons experiences, enabling you to help each other understand and accept your behaviors. During our therapy sessions, we will then go into these different behavior patterns and try as best we can to interpret them. Now, do either of you have any questions."

Arthur started to ask a question, but Carlee jumped in. "How detailed do you want us to get? Gory and personal?"

"That and more," Dr. Brookfield said. "If you experienced it, reveal it to me and to your husband. We must be prepared to deal with the consequences of any trauma."

"No more questions," Carlee said, looking a little overwhelmed.

"I know it's a lot to consider, but it's important to your health, Carlee."

When they got off of the phone, Arthur pulled Carlee down to the floor and waited until she was settled.

"I don't want to surprise you when you hear everything," he said, even though he was reluctant to tell all. "First, you are going to learn things about me of which I am totally ashamed, embarrassed and would like to not go there with the counselor, but I am prepared to as long as you know how I feel about what I did."

Carlee looked at him but did not smile. "We will deal with the consequences, so tell all and let us get past this."

"My behavior was gross for a short time in my life. Do you want me to start now or wait until the counselor is present?"

Carlee thought it over. "We should wait for the counselor so we do not get in over our heads." She reached for his hand. "But I can handle it. Trust me."

***

The counselor was very professional and friendly. She explained her background and gave her qualifications. After everyone was comfortably settled in, she looked directly at Carlee.

"We have something in common," she said, hoping to break the ice. "My first name is also Carlee. Carlee Brookfield." She turned to Arthur and asked, "Who is willing to talk first?"

Arthur's face flushed. "Since I have the greatest degree of reluctance, perhaps I should go first and get it behind us."

Dr. Brookfield looked at Carlee, and she nodded.

Arthur shifted in his chair. "I been extremely hesitant to tell Carlee everything. However, I truly love my wife, and I am prepared to be candid and to deal with the consequences.

"As you know, I was an Air Traffic Control Supervisor at O'Hare in Chicago for ten years before I was forced into medical retirement. After I left my job, I quickly got another one but found it to be menial, not satisfactory. I quit after three weeks. This started a pattern of job-hopping. While at the tower, I would periodically drink Jack Daniel's and 7 Up. Soon, I started drinking every night and some times during the day." He looked down at the floor and cleared his throat.

"Again, I want to tell you how difficult this is. For a period of time, I did horrible and disgusting things. My behavior was almost unspeakable. I am so ashamed. For a while, I tried traveling to see the country to keep my mind occupied. I went back to Denver, my home town, and then to Las Vegas, to Los Angeles and points in between.

"After about two years I returned to Chicago. Again, I got a menial job, and this time, I met a lady on the job that was having a difficult time performing the functions assigned to her. She was of a mix ethnically—I think African American and Hispanic and

French. She was a nice person, but the supervisor at work did not like her and kept telling her she was an idiot and could not learn simple functions. I kept having flash-backs to the demeaning approach I had observed at the control tower.

"During a break, she confided in me that she worried about her daughter while she was at work and found it difficult to concentrate. I told her I was going to help her. We agreed I would accompany her to her apartment, and we would review the functions required at work. We intended to keep doing this until she knew them well enough to perform each function in an outstanding manner. Within a week, her job performance improved tremendously. She even received a pay increase. We became good friends.

"I drove thirty-five miles to work each day and then returned to my apartment each night. She—Alice is her name—Alice suggested I move in with her, pay part of the food bill and keep teaching her at night so she would continue to get better at her job. At first, I did not want to, but Alice and I started liking each other. One night, I had a difficult time at work because the supervisor got all over a guy that was not fully functional and hit the guy. I intervened and told the supervisor to not ever do that again. He swung at me and missed. I told him if he tried that again, he would be turned in to the owner of the shop. I then walked out, went to the liquor store and bought a quart of Jack Daniels and a six-pack of 7 Up.

"When I got to Alice's apartment, Denise, the daughter invited me in and then went to bed on the couch. I had several drinks. Alice came home, and we had more drinks. We had sex that night while her ten-year-old daughter slept on the couch in the same room we were in."

Carlee let out a small gasp and looked at Dr. Brookfield for guidance.

The counselor shook her head and said, "Be aware that what you tell me next may mean I will have to report your behavior."

"Oh no," Arthur said quickly. "Denise was asleep. I didn't touch her." Carlee looked relieved.

"Sometime in the afternoon, I went back to my employer and talked to the supervisor. He was apologetic, and so was I, so we cleared things up between us. Then the supervisor asked about Alice. He said he wanted her back there to work and, if I could get her back, he would see to it that she was taken care of. I promised him I would talk to her.

"The next night, I went to Alice's apartment around 9:30 p.m. Alice was taking something—some kind of pills—and drinking alcohol. She gave me one of the pills, and I took it.

"After quitting my job, I decided to travel. Last time, I had gone west to Los Angeles. This time, I traveled to New York and made my way to Niagara Falls. I remember seeing the most beautiful scenery in the world. On my way back through Michigan—I do not remember the city or highway—I stopped at a bar and picked up a woman that was tending bar and serving as a waitress. I returned to my car, checked my wallet and confirmed the money was still there, and then I drove toward Chicago. When I got home, I recalled what I had done. Depression overwhelmed me, and I found myself in the Des Plaines hospital where I was treated and then released. I went to my apartment and tried to overcome my depression.

"There is one other time when my behavior became obnoxiously abhorrent, and I want to know if I must tell about this."

The counselor replied, "If you want to heal, you must tell all of it."

Arthur took a long drink of water and asked, "First, can I confirm none of this will ever be made known to anyone?"

Dr. Brookfield said, "I will confirm that no one is privileged to this information unless it involves a minor. Please proceed."

Arthur then shook his head. "I'm not feeling well."

The counselor stood and said, "I think we need to take a break. Why don't you get some coffee or a soda, and I'll see you back here in fifteen minutes."

Carlee was silent during the break, refusing to talk to Arthur. When they returned to Dr. Brookfield's office, Carlee was asked to share her experiences.

"I wrote them down, and I've already gone over them with Arthur. Can I just give you a copy?"

"Is that alright with you, Arthur?"

He agreed.

"We are ahead of the game, then Carlee. No need to say it again.

"The next step is to review the important events, those that continue to impact your life today. Since I have not heard Carlee's experiences as of today, I will need to read them, which I will do before we meet again. I will ask each of you questions, and I will expect you to respond honestly and candidly. That will determine the action I will propose in order that we deal effectively with each important occurrence. First, Arthur, are there questions you might have regarding Carlee's experiences?"

Arthur said, "Yes, I have some that need to be addressed."

The counselor nodded for him to continue.

"When someone fails to achieve complete certification at the O'Hare Control Tower, and it is partly due to inhumane, demeaning and insulting treatment at the hands of their instructor—which I believe occurred in Carlee's situation—can this cause severe mental trauma for years following the termination of training?"

Dr. Brookfield nodded. "Certainly. Air traffic control is stressful to begin with. The added anguish of being mistreated can be very damaging."

"And when a young lady is also called demeaning names, does that add to the emotional damage?"

The counselor replied, "Yes, absolutely."

"Not only was Carlee called vulgar names, she had been hassled by other women in the facility because she was a virgin."

"That type of trauma can be totally detrimental to any recovery. I am not certain the degree of damage to one's self-esteem, and cannot assess the overall effect until I spend more time with Carlee. However, I will take this as an action item for us to deal with."

Arthur said, "I have one more question. As you may know, Carlee and I were recently married. Can the damage that has occurred in Carlee's case result in her inability to enjoy or achieve sexual satisfaction when having sex with her partner?"

"Healing can occur with proper therapy." With that, Dr. Brookfield suggested they scheduled their next appointment and stop for the day.

***

Arthur and Carlee were enjoying their new home, but they soon learned there were many facets of life they each wanted to know. The absences and experiences they each encountered had taken their toll, and they were asking the counselor to help them bridge the gaps in their understanding of each other. Some of their conversations led to misconceptions or perceptions of each other that were both good and bad. Yet, together the two made a lovely couple deeply involved in a beautiful yet complex relationship.

Carlee was also reconnecting with her parents, and Arthur was beginning that part of their lives anew. His savvy purchase of the house convinced Carlee's parents that Arthur was a good provider and caused them to readily accept their new son-in-law. Mr. and Mrs. Jenkins threw a lovely party while Eileen and her husband were still visiting, giving the three families an opportunity to bond. Carlee was becoming less and less stressed and demonstrated genuine gratitude for the happenings of late, and Arthur saw that his initiative was beginning to have a positive effect on Carlee.

She had recently weighed in at the doctor's office, and the scales showed a healthy increase in weight. Arthur was aware that his attention to those things were important to help reduce stress. His years as a controller and supervisor taught him to plan and strategize, using diplomacy yet firmness when necessary, in his dealing with people. He believed Carlee had been thrown to the wolves for years and that now was time for her to wake up each morning expecting the best life could offer.

***

The counselor was very perceptive, and Arthur and Carlee had become fond of Mrs. Brookfield. They were beginning to trust her more with each meeting. Still, due to the serious nature of Arthur's past, they were making slow progress. Mrs. Brookfield was patient and very determined to help the couple through their problems.

Early in their relationship, Arthur had been most apprehensive about his past sordid behavior—something that still caused him shame. Now, he wanted to get that part of his life behind him. While he was concerned about Mrs. Brookfield's reaction, he was more worried about what Carlee might think of him but not be willing to say out loud. Carlee was his wife, the love of Arthur's life, and he genuinely cared what she thought about him.

Arthur was also aware that there could be consequences both legally and for his relationship with Carlee. He worried what she might decide to do, but he would have to wait and see what came to the surface in Carlee's sessions. He had to admit that, despite his own transgressions, he was a jealous person and worried just how he would handle finding out that his wife might have been with other men. As hypocritical as it was, he wanted a pure and clean, untouched woman for his own.

At their next session, Arthur reluctantly listened to Dr. Brookfield's assessment and recommendations. She summarized what she knew of Carlee's experiences and recommended that Carlee gain more insight into Arthur's behavior.

"I see nothing significantly troubling about Carlee's behavior over the past ten years aside from Carlee's decision to avoid sexual intercourse in the past and her feelings of apprehension regarding her desire or lack thereof," the counselor said. "Is this still an issue?"

Carlee blushed. "Not as of late. You will need to ask Arthur if things are good."

Dr. Brookfield looked at Arthur.

He nodded slightly and replied, "Things are good, and so is Carlee."

"Then we need to turn to your issues, Arthur. I want to explore what led to your behavior after you left your controller position. You have made it clear you are convinced the FAA took action they did not have to take because they needed a fall guy relating to the accident between DL42 and NC 81. Can you be more specific, perhaps elaborate briefly on the details of what occurred?"

Arthur took a minute to recall the event. "The weather that evening was horrible. Fog, light rain and extremely poor visibility sometimes as low as zero to a sixteenth of a mile. Traffic was very heavy for each controller. The ground controller was responsible for issuing instructions to pilots who were taxiing to and from the runways. He did not have benefit of a ground radar to let him know where each aircraft was within the system. The Airport Surveillance Detection Equipment was inoperative during the evening shift and of no use to the controller.

"Taxiway zebra exists between runway 32R and 32L run-up pads and ultimately between the two runways. The O'Hare Control Tower Supervisor, due to wind conditions and operational efficiency, decided to land and depart on both parallel runways 14L and 14R and Runway 27L. We had been on that runway configuration for about three hours. When DL 42 landed on runway 14L and exited at the end of the runway, the pilot was effectively on the runway 32R run-up pad. Meanwhile departing aircraft were taxiing to runway 14L, 14R and 27L for departure. This configuration was the most productive of the configurations available to the supervisor that evening. It allowed the maximum number of aircraft possible to be active going to and from the runways. It also placed the maximum number of aircraft into the system that was possible. This created frequency congestion, blocked transmissions from the ground controller to pilot and from the pilot to the ground controller, thereby preventing either pilot or ground controller from participating in clear, unobstructed conversation at a critical time.

"When DL42 cleared runway 14L, the pilot taxied beyond the runway 32R run-up pad which would have been the norm, and reported a gate delay to the ground controller. The controller told the pilot to just pull over to the 32 run-up pad and call when he had a gate assigned. The DL42 pilot, knowing he was beyond the 32R run-up pad when he received instructions from the ground controller, proceeded to taxi his aircraft to the runway 32L run-up.

In order to do this, DL42 had to cross runway 27L which was being utilized as a departing runway.

"At this time, DL42 was traversing a route that would conflict with crossing departures on runway 27L and technically should have been issued hold instructions. DL 42 was not issued those instructions and crossed runway 27L while NC 81 was in a departing configuration. The ground controller also issued incomplete taxi instructions to the pilot of DL42 when he told DL 42 just to pull over to the 32 run-up pad. He should have said, D42 pull over to the 32R run-up pad and inform me when you have received a gate assignment. Neither pilot of either aircraft observed the other, and they collided, killing more than 32 passengers and crew.

"NC81 came to rest on runway 32L facing the Northwesterly direction. Fire department personnel happened to see the crash and reported it to the ground controller. They assisted emergency equipment in trying to find the crash site as the visibility was severely limited. The fire department responded and was on the scene within two minutes of the disaster. Since there was inoperative equipment in the tower that would have normally been used by the ground controller, his mistake in issuing incorrect instructions would have been corrected by the ground controller as he would have observed DL42 taxi beyond the run-up pad. He would have questioned his intent, thereby preventing him from taxiing across runway 27L.

"I'm positive that this failure of equipment caused the accident. The FAA decided the ground controller was at fault and ended his career," Arthur said, bowing his head. "I feel sick every time I think of the injustice of it all. I want to curse and do harm to the people who did this to me. Instead, I walked the earth in pain and tried to deal with my conscience. I even became so disheartened that I wanted to get revenge. Unfortunately, I took that revenge out on the wrong people."

"Trauma effects different people differently," Mrs. Brookfield said.

"I need this to preserve a good life for Carlee and me." Arthur looked at Carlee who was crying. "I truly apologize for my past behavior." He was completely wet from perspiration and totally fatigued. He uttered softly but firmly, "Carlee, God knows I love you."

Mrs. Brookfield took a moment before responding. "The response to your sense of failure is rooted in normal behavior, historically. But that does not excuse the harm you may have caused others. Your own sense of morality led to much of your suffering.

"While Carlee's behavior was highly influenced by her medical condition—primarily MS—you, Arthur, were driven by your sense of failure to achieve something you wanted and needed to maintain your self-image. This continues to seriously impact your life. We need to resolve the true issue that haunts you."

Mrs. Brookfield asked, "Carlee, do you have a question for me or Arthur?"

Carlee's cheeks flushed, and then she looked at Arthur. "Since we have been having sex, are you satisfied?"

Arthur grabbed her hands and nodded. "I have never thought of anyone else since we got back together."

Mrs. Brookfield then asked, "It is my opinion that your basic value system has not been destroyed, however it has been severely damaged and could be subject to a small degree of vindictive behavior on the part of either party if you suspected each other. Both of you have experienced significant trauma. This can cause sensitive nerves, overreaction to certain stimuli, and unpleasant action by either person. If you are careful and avoid giving one or the other an opportunity to be vindictive, I suspect you can heal from this and enjoy a loving relationship."

She leaned back in her chair. "I want to meet with each of you separately once a week for the next six months. Meanwhile, Carlee, I will be particularly interested in your energy level and progress in treating the MS disease. For now, go enjoy life, and try to be as open with each other as possible these next few weeks."

***

Arthur and Carlee left the Counselor's office and began to face the unknown world of medical intrigue, research and options that did not appear to hold much hope for Carlee. Arthur was mildly depressed having just opened himself clearly and completely to the woman he loved. He was not at all sure how much degradation she could handle without letting it adversely affect her image of him. Arthur was worried, but he was also determined to fix it.

"Sweetheart, I commit to you a hundred percent. I will never betray you or our values as a couple for as long as I live. Please believe me. None of what you heard from me today will ever happen again, ever."

Carlee grabbed Arthur and hugged him. "Take me home," she said, hoping for privacy before she let the tears fall.

The next day, Arthur woke up emotionally drained and wanted to perform menial work in the yard as it needed attention. The previous owner had done a great job. Consequently, the grass needed to be mowed and trimmed. Arthur decided he wanted a manicured lawn and, now that he had a chance for one, he was going to enjoy it.

In the middle of the afternoon, a hot southwest sun beamed down on him. He realized he should have done the difficult work in the early morning hours. When he started toward the garage, he saw Carlee sprawled on a blanket enjoying freshly cut grass. She was irresistible, and he could not stop himself from joining her. They lounged on the lawn for a while and talked about the dream that seemed to be coming true. Neither of them thought of Chicago or the consequences of their experiences.

They did discuss the appointments they had made for the next day, including Carlee's first with the neurologist in Albuquerque. She asked if Arthur was going to come with her.

"Absolutely," he said. "I will attend any and all of your medical appointments as long as you are comfortable with me there."

"It's boring and full of tests, tests and more tests," she said.

"You are enough excitement for me." He leaned over and kissed her on the lips.

"Is that supposed to be humor?"

Arthur shrugged and said, "I tried."

The following day, the neurologist was professional and courteous, and provided enough information for both of them to review before the next appointment. She scheduled a battery of tests and asked for Carlee's medical records.

"I believe good things will come from the new treatments available. The most important thing is to get an accurate diagnosis as to how far the disease has progressed, and to make sure you follow the carefully-developed care plan we set up for you."

Arthur and Carlee had heard most of this before, but they were paying close attention to her words. They were specifically interested in the effect MS might have on a woman trying to get pregnant.

"We will be taking a close look at Carlee's condition to ensure against a misdiagnosis such as Lupus, brain infections, multiple strokes or other conditions involving the central nervous system.

I'll develop a detailed medical history that included members of the family as well." She suggested they pay close attention to behavioral health issues including depression, mood swings and even thoughts of suicide. "Do not keep these feelings or thoughts to yourself," she warned. "Even you, Arthur."

She looked back at Carlee. "Confusion can occur and if it does or it increases, I should know about it. Rest and sleep when you need it to reduce stress, however, if you seem to be sleepy after getting adequate sleep, I want to be informed. These are but a few of the issues we will be monitoring. I encourage you to become an expert in your own care."

Carlee asked, "Does MS adversely affected a woman's ability to become pregnant?"

"Not normally. In unusual circumstances, the woman might experience difficulties due to fatigue, stress or some other factor that affects conception. It might help to confirm that Arthur is fertile. Too often, couples come up against this issue after years of trying for a child."

Arthur and Carlee walked to the elevator and headed to the first-floor lab for Carlee's scheduled MRI. While they waited, they discussed Arthur's role in helping Carlee. Arthur noticed an element of sensitivity when he asked questions. It seemed that so many of the treatments were certain, always subjective. When he thought about it, he realized he should settle down and think of Carlee, not Arthur.

On their way home, they stopped at a furniture store. Prior to this, if they wanted something they bought it without much consideration, but when they calculated the cost of furnishing a house, they had to plan ahead.

On the way home Carlee asked, "Do you think I will ever be able to get my license again and drive a car?"

"I do not understand why you cannot drive now," Arthur said. "What happened that caused you to lose your license in the first place?"

Carlee lowered her eyes. "At one time in my life, I would faint and become unconscious."

"That would do it. How long has it been since that occurred."

"Two years."

"We should discuss this with the Neurologist. If it's been that long, maybe you have stabalized."

The next day, they attended church with Carlee's parents. Afterward, the four of them went to lunch at a nice restaurant. During their conversion, Arthur mentioned the need for exercise equipment to help Carlee keep her strength up.

"What are you looking for?" Bill asked.

Arthur explained the items that would do Carlee the most good. "I just don't know what we can afford at this point. We've invested a great deal already in the purchase of the house."

Bill suggested they rent to buy as a strategy. He told his daughter later that Arthur seemed like a good conservative when it came to money, and he was sure they would always have the money they needed to live comfortably.

The couple found a good deal on used equipment and had it delivered on Monday.

They attended their scheduled therapy session with the neurologist. Carlee reported the preparation for her exercise program including the purchase of equipment.

"That's great," Dr. Brookfield said. "Today I'd like to talk more about the issues you had with the other women who made derogatory remarks when you were working the control tower."

Carlee said, "I think of the comments periodically, but mostly I think of the way the comments made me feel. I thought I was a prude having lived for over twenty years without a sexual experience. But I wanted to remain pure for my future husband. Sometimes I did wonder if I was choosing the right path. I will admit it seemed they were having fun, especially when they bragged about what they did and how many times."

Mrs. Brookfield asked, "Do you feel different about it today?"

Carlee said, "Somewhat. I have recently initiated sexual activity similar to what I understood the women did back then. Some of it is okay, some of it is terrific and some of it is not worth doing."

"Are you uncomfortable talking about it?"

Carlee said, "I know it's part of the process we are following, and it is okay."

The counselor turned to Arthur. "What thoughts do either of you have about what happened to you while at the O'Hare Control Tower?"

Arthur became agitated. "I am upset because of the injustice that caused my separation from the FAA in late 1968." He calmed a bit and added, "It's frustrating that the truth was glossed over in favor of maintaining a good front for the public."

"Do you want to explore that further?"

"Not right now," Arthur admitted. "I'd rather focus these sessions on Carlee's issues."

Dr. Brookfield turned to Carlee. "And you?"

"The name calling still haunts me today," she said. "Because I was forced to endure being called filthy and derogatory names while my work associates were present, and that ultimately caused me to be terminated from the very job that I enjoyed, I get angry every time I think of what occurred. I felt so helpless."

Dr. Brookfield looked sympathetically at her. "That is exactly the type of stress you don't need with your illness. We will need to work on these issues for your overall recovery. Do you know why you reacted the way you did?"

Carlee reacted with the same anger as Arthur had earlier. "If it had been you, Dr. Brookfield, a woman, would you have appreciated being teased about your sex life with the guys and then have your training instructor call you a cunt? Would you have liked being terminated from your job because of a poor performance working a radar position you knew very well how to perform?" Carlee, red faced again, sat down and said, "I'm through."

Dr. Brookfield looked at them both. "I appreciate your candor. Thank you."

***

After learning the exercise routines prescribed by Carlee's physician, Carlee and Arthur committed themselves to extensive and daily work out activities designed to develop physical strength, endurance and reduction of stress. The plan was a gradual one as it took into consideration the issues Carlee was trying to deal with as a MS patient. For Arthur, the exercises were not strenuous but, as they progressed, he could feel them challenge his stamina. He was pleased with the equipment purchases and the throw rugs that provided color and style to their basement. They quickly added a TV, stereo and a couch to accommodate either of them on those days where exercise did not seem to be the thing to do. Sometimes the couch won the argument without ever speaking a word.

Carlee was required to keep documentation of her exercise routines, and Arthur kept his own documentation just to support his wife's efforts. The physician asked to keep tabs on Carlee's notes.

"Generally speaking, I, as your physician, don't just want to know how you are doing. It is important that I know."

***

Carlee and Arthur could now focus on dealing with their current emotional growth. The neurologist was impressed with Carlee's progress and suggested she continue her diet and exercise program, and continued to monitor her control of MS which was progressing better every day.

The counselor expressed concern with Arthur's lack of progress in letting go of the past and his need to look to the future with too much optimism.

"I miss the challenge and sense of achievement I experienced from working live air traffic," he admitted. "Air traffic controllers have always been extremely confident of their abilities to accomplish anything."

With their regular physician, Arthur turned the subject to Carlee's desire to become pregnant.

"Is there anything she needs to do that she was not currently doing?"

The physician said, "I'll review the results in your files, but I do recall anything that stood out from the previous tests. Maybe it will just take a little patience."

Arthur looked at Carlee and said, "I think I will take you on a long vacation to the beach. That should help matters for both me and you."

Carlee's smile was approval enough.

At the counselor's, Arthur was bold. "I believe Carlee and I need a break from trying to solve problems we have been unable to identify. When they do surface, we will deal with them head on. But now I believe we just need to play husband and wife around the house for thirty days or so and then resume."

Dr. Brookfield smiled. "I don't see what this would hurt. And it just might help. I will schedule your next appointment a month out."

Carlee and Arthur said their thanks and departed for home.

***

The car was packed, full of fuel, and Carlee and Arthur were ready to travel. They planned to drive to the outskirts of San Diego, get a motel, eat at a great restaurant and enjoy a full night of restful sleep. They planned the rest of their vacation. The weather was beautiful and they had no worries or concerns except the day to day problems of where to eat and where to stop for the night. They did not have a date to return, nor did they want to think of one. They were free to do anything or nothing.

They arrived at the first motel after dark. They slept late the next morning, but it was even later when they left the motel. They drove around San Diego, enjoying the scenery and relaxing—precisely what the doctors had ordered. Arthur believed Carlee was enjoying their time together, and he committed again to a stress-free vacation. They walked on the sandy beaches and played in the cool water of the Pacific Ocean. When a more serious subject arose, Carlee became irritated and told Arthur to shut up.

Early the next day, Dr. Brookfield called Arthur and asked for a status report of Carlee's progress. Arthur left the motel room so he could speak openly with the counselor.

"I'm very concerned," Arthur said. "Carlee has abandoned her health routine and started behaving in a manner that's hard to describe. I try to talk to her about it, but she gets angry and shuts me down. She actually asked me for a divorce last night."

Dr. Brookfield was shocked to hear the news. "Perhaps you should return home. I'll give you a couple of days, and then I'll call Carlee."

A few days later, Carlee asked Arthur to go with her at Dr. Brookfield's office. He was still reeling from the change in his wife. He still loved Carlee and reflected back over several years to Chicago, Idaho, and the Mayo Clinic. As he reflected, he prayed to God for guidance and began to think of the future.

Dr. Brookfield's receptionist escorted the two of them to a conference room which was occupied by an administrative person who was going to take notes of the conversation. When the counselor entered the room, she was followed by her husband, Carlee's personal physician and a woman introduced as a specialist in dealing with MS. Dr. Brookfield began by asking Carlee to provide a current status of her health, her attitude and her well- being.

Carlee began to cry. Arthur comforted her and assured her she was among friends.

"Can you give us an update on how you are feeling, Carlee?"

She rubbed her hands before taking a deep breath. "I just can't control my anger anymore. I eat all of the wrong things, and the stress is as bad as when I was in the hospital in Chicago."

"What do you suggest?" Arthur asked.

"I seriously want a divorce," Carlee admitted. "I thought I could live with your past, Arthur. But I was wrong. You won't confront it."

Arthur looked at Dr. Brookfield. "What do I do?"

"For Carlee's health, I must suggest a separation. You both need to work through your issues, but perhaps you need to do so as individuals."

Arthur glared at his wife. "The issue isn't with the relationship. The issue is MS and I cannot fix that." He walked out of the conference room.

Wager to Romance

On a cold and windy night on January 8, 1995, during a flight from Los Angeles to Chicago, Robert Glasco sat in the aisle seat and waited patiently for someone to occupy the window seat. He took a one-dollar bill from his wallet. A mechanical engineer, he was returning from a business trip and was somewhat bored with it all. The dollar bill was to serve as a communication starter with whoever occupied the window seat. As additional passengers boarded the airplane, a beautiful woman asked if she could be excused as she had the window.

Once she had settled in, Robert held up the bill and said, "I'm betting a dollar that we luck out, and no one occupies the center seat."

The lady smiled warily, but then said, "I'll take that wager. Hi. I'm Ellen Blakely."

Robert, a confirmed bachelor, instantly noticed the beauty of Ellen's eyes and smile. Even though he would not, at this stage of their acquaintance, admit his attraction to her, he could not deny it.

Soon a gentleman approached and looked at Robert. "Excuse me, but I have the middle seat."

Robert stood to let the man pass, and then he handed Ellen his one dollar bill.

Before the newcomer could get comfortable, Ellen asked the gentlemen if he would prefer the window seat.

"Thank you," he said, and they traded places.

Ellen's smile was contagious. As the threesome rearranged their newly assigned seats, Ellen made it clear to Robert that she wanted to return the dollar bill as if their bet had become null and void. The two of them talked the remainder of the flight, except for a period when Ellen snoozed lightly with her head resting on Robert's shoulder. He found her perfume intoxicating.

Robert was a dedicated business associate of a mechanical engineering firm. He had been totally committed to his job, reaching for success above all—until Ellen came along. Confused by what he considered a distraction, it was all he could do to refrain from holding her hand or even kissing her, but he was moved to do something.

When she woke from her nap, he quietly proposed they meet after they landed in Chicago and get better acquainted. Ellen smiled and accepted immediately.

Once they left the plane, the couple walked to baggage claim together.

"Can I take you to lunch?" Robert asked.

Ellen turned the tables. "I would like to invite *you* to lunch. I know a place," she said.

Robert accepted. Once they'd collected their suitcases, she led him to the street where a limo was waiting. The driver opened a door for the couple and then stowed their luggage in the trunk.

"Nice car," Robert said, running his hand over the leather seat.

"It's the company's. I'm an exec for a mechanical engineering company."

They managed a comfortable conversation over a lengthy lunch, and Ellen insisted she—or her company—pick up the tab. After she had paid, she apologized for having to break away and file a report on the latest trip. The two exchanged personal information, and Ellen insisted that her driver deliver Robert to his home.

"Next time," he said, "we should meet somewhere less formal."

"Tomorrow night?" she asked. After watching the look of surprise spread across Robert's face, she added, "Your place. And you're cooking."

At Robert's door the next evening, Ellen appeared with a bottle of very expensive wine in hand. "Something to inspire our discussion of mechanical engineering."

"Not tonight," Robert said. "No work. Just you and I getting to know each other."

They discussed many things, but when it came to personal histories, Ellen would often redirect her comments to her travels throughout the U.S., Canada, Mexico and the European Union for work. Work was her passion.

They ended the evening on a high note and agreed to meet again over the weekend. When they returned to their respective businesses on Monday, each had trouble concentrating on work and the priorities before them. Frustrated by the distraction, Ellen quickly made it clear that she did not want to continue any meaningful relationship with Robert.

***

During work hours the next few months, Ellen remained quiet about visits to her obstetrician. The only one who knew her situation was her mother, Kathleen Howser.

"I don't know if I can do this," Ellen had admitted early in the pregnancy.

"You are not having an abortion," her mother insisted. "I will raise the child myself."

After agonizing over her decision for months, Ellen relinquished the right to raise her son. She was too dedicated to her the firm and her work. She needed to stay focused and to allow her mother to be the actual mom.

Ellen had been educated at Georgetown University, majoring in mechanical engineering with a minor in religious studies. She had never married. However, she frequently dated well-to-do gentlemen and traveled whenever the opportunity presented itself. She was driven to succeed and made the Dean's List every semester while in college. After leaving the collegiate environment, she became extremely successful as a part owner and influential member of the Blakely, Bakefield, and Drone Contracting firm specializing in engineering construction. At thirty-eight, she dedicated herself to work above anything else.

Ellen was informal among work associates and fostered perfection in the performance of assigned duties. She was a beautiful woman, standing five feet ten inches tall with strawberry blonde hair, blue eyes and a beautiful smile. Single by choice, she chose her closest male friends carefully. She was a private person who did not often participate in social interaction. In her spare time, she read many books, studied the most current mechanical engineering books and magazines, and subscribed to a local readers club of which she was an officer. Her book preference generally leaned toward religious or moralistic subjects. It seemed to her that her work life was fulfillment enough.

Robert Glasco, the only child of Mr. and Mrs. Clifford Glasco, was educated at Stanford University and played football where he was successful at the position of tight end. His six-foot four-inch frame benefited him greatly. He was a strong, muscled, and a physical man who enjoyed competition. This competitive nature ultimately helped him in his chosen profession of mechanical engineering. He was a quiet and reserved person who seldom dated, although he demonstrated ultimate respect whenever he was in their company.

He was frequently asked to accompany ladies to social events, yet he seldom accepted their invitation.

Despite this, he often thought of Ellen and their weekend together. Over the years, he had been tempted to contact her, but honored her surprising request to avoid further encounters.

One day at work, Robert was informed by the administrative assistant that he had earned enough time off that he would lose some it if he did not take a vacation. Accordingly, he booked a vacation at a resort in the Bahamas and scheduled a flight. While there, he lounged on the beach, ate delicious food, and drank the best wine available. He met several available women but, when he engaged them in conversation, he was not impressed and moved on.

On the third day of his vacation, he remembered Ellen and wondered if he should go against her desire to disconnect. The more he thought of her wishes, the more it irritated him, yet he could not get her out of his mind. For some reason, he thought he should be able to discipline himself—to control his mind—but then he considered this kind of thinking too emotional.

Ellen often thought of Robert, especially as she watched her son Sheldon grow up. Though she did not know for sure who the father was, it could have been Robert. Their encounter had been so brief and the pregnancy had happened so quickly.

Her mother pushed for a DNA test, but Ellen was too independent to yield to her mother for anything. She loved her mother, but it was one of those things that got under Ellen's skin. Besides, Sheldon was in college now and dating a beautiful young lady that adored him. She wanted to know who the father was, but she wasn't willing to disrupt Sheldon's life at this point.

One sunny afternoon, Sheldon introduced his fiancé, Brenda. "Mother," he said to Kathleen, "we want to get married right after graduation."

For the first time in her life, Ellen was jealous of her mother. She had to keep her comments to herself—choking back tears, but she was very proud of the way her mother had raised her baby. For a moment, Ellen thought of Robert, and another tear rolled down her cheek. Again she thought of a DNA test, just to be sure.

Ellen was reluctant to ask Sheldon for a blood sample. Finally, she came up with the proper excuse, and Sheldon agreed without hesitation. They accompanied each other to see Ellen's doctor, and it was over in less than ten minutes. Next—to get a sample from Robert.

Ellen called Robert and asked if the two of them could have lunch.

"Of course," he said. "When do you suggest?"

"How about tomorrow at eleven, if that is okay with you."

At the restaurant, Ellen broke the ice first. "I have a question for you, but I need to know that you won't be angry."

Robert looked concerned and said, "I would imagine it will depend on the question."

They ordered their meal, and then Ellen leaned in to ask, "How would you feel about being a father?"

At first, Robert seemed baffled. Soon a look of recognition came over his face. The weekend after we met?"

She nodded. "I want to have a DNA test done to be sure."

For a long moment, Ellen couldn't read Robert's emotions. At last, he asked, "Do you want it to be me?"

"I do."

"And what if I'm not the father?" He reached across the table and tried to take her hand, but she pulled back. He watched her tear up before adding, "I have wished all these years that we had stayed connected. I've never met another woman I considered marrying."

"So, you'll take the test?" she asked at last.

"Yes," he said.

For the rest of the meal, the two relaxed into an old familiarity. They managed a comfortable hug when they left.

***

A week later, Robert met Ellen at her doctor's for the test, and it was done in less than ten minutes. "Please let me know as soon as you find out," he told her.

Three weeks later, Ellen called with the results. "Sheldon is your son," she said. Where do you want to go from here?"

"Can I take you to dinner? We should probably discuss how to tell Sheldon."

"Or *if* we tell him."

Robert chose a high-end restaurant with low light and a quiet atmosphere. They seemed to enjoy their time and the recollection of their lives over the many years since that fateful weekend. Finally, he asked, "Why did you suspect it was me?"

"I'm not a promiscuous woman. There were only two choices."

"You know I've always loved you," he said, catching her off guard.

At the end of their meal, Robert asked if he could meet his son.

"I need to talk to my mother first," Ellen said. "And then I'll have to have a conversation with Sheldon to prepare him for the news. I don't know how he will take it."

She called her mother the next day and discussed her and Robert's conversation. "Are you okay with this?"

"I have to be," Kathleen said. "It's long overdue."

They scheduled a lunch with Sheldon on the University of Illinois campus. He asked if he could bring his fiancé Brenda, and they agreed that would be fine.

Introductions were made, and everyone seemed initially at ease.

"What's your major?" Robert asked when they were seated.

"Animal Husbandry with a minor in Finance and Banking."

Robert turned to Brenda and asked her the same question.

Her blue eyes sparkled with optimism and eagerness when she answered. "Plant Science with a minor in Finance and Banking."

The party of five tried to play catch up for the years they had missed. Sheldon was particularly interested in Robert's occupation, and he asked numerous questions. Later, he informed the group that he and Brenda were planning a wedding after graduation. They were going to work for a large Angus breeding farm to learn first-hand the pros and cons of running a Registered Angus operation.

Brenda spoke up. "My plan is to operate a large greenhouse, marketing plants to smaller nurseries."

Kathleen turned to Sheldon. "How are you planning to finance the Angus farm?"

"A little at a time," he admitted. "I've worked with several breeding operators and listened to their views concerning several issues that could affect a successful operation. I have been offered a position in two of the larger operations if I only wanted to become an employee. I'll do that to get started. And Brenda will support me at first. Once the operation is underway, she can turn her attention to the green house and market those nurseries that did not have the space to always produce what they needed."

Sheldon then looked at Robert and asked, "Are you and Ellen planning to build a relationship? It seems the two of you have so much to offer each other."

Robert was surprised that Sheldon called his mother by her first name, but he didn't press the issue. "I have always loved Ellen and would be open to spending more time together and then see where it takes us." He looked questioningly at Ellen. "Perhaps you would take a trip to Europe with me."

She didn't answer right away, but then said, "I would need to schedule vacation time. It won't be easy."

Robert was happy she hadn't dismissed the idea outright.

***

Robert sat alone in his study and poured over the travel information he had obtained. He thought back to Ellen's comment—*it won't be easy*—and decided to call and ask what she was referring to.

Ellen answered on the first ring and seemed thrilled that Robert had called.

"Hey," he said after they had exchanged pleasantries. "What did you mean when you said it wouldn't be easy to get vacation time?"

"Oh. Well, I wanted to keep Sheldon from expecting too much too soon. He's always wanted to see me married to someone. But don't worry. I've already talked to the company about time off. Where and when do you want to go?"

Robert suggested they lunch at his place and review some of the travel brochures he had picked up. After they hung up, he began cleaning the bachelor pad he called home. He bought wine and fresh food from the local deli.

The doorbell rang, and he jumped. Ellen stood in the doorway as beautiful as could be—her image enhanced by Robert's anticipation. "Uh, come in," he said, stepping back from the doorway.

He escorting her to the dining room invited her to sit. "I hope you are ready to enjoy a bachelor's brunch."

Ellen moved toward Robert and gave him a very passionate hug and kiss before she sat down. Robert served juice, water and coffee, and began passing the food when Ellen asked if they could stop and return thanks for their nourishment.

"Certainly," Robert agreed.

They ate and drank and talked for more than four hours before moving to the living room. They both expressed their regrets for missing over twenty-five years of each other's lives, and neither could explain how or why it happened. It just did. Robert asked about the future and wondered if he had any serious competition.

"Yes," Ellen said, jokingly. "My business to which I am addicted." When Robert let out a sigh of relief, Ellen put him at ease, saying, "I have not seen another man in ten years and do not plan to look for one."

Robert gave her a hug and asked if she would commit to taking an extended vacation with him. "I've been looking into Moscow or Switzerland or London."

They talked over the options, and then Robert asked about Sheldon and his goals.

"You should spend time with him," Ellen said. "He is a deep-thinking gentleman." She talked about what a wonderful job her mother had done raising him. "And Brenda is almost a copy of Sheldon."

They discussed their businesses and promised to meet again during the evening hour and invite Sheldon and Brenda to dinner. They gave each other passionate kisses as they parted.

Dinning was a pleasure for everyone. The food was delicious and the company interesting. Robert genuinely wanted to get to know his son, and Sheldon wanted to get to know his father. They learned they had much in common.

Again, Sheldon brought up the idea of working with the Angus breeding operation that he was currently familiar with. He also said he had been reviewing advertisements that provided the opportunity to purchase an on-going operation if the opportunity ever presented itself.

"Are you thinking of a large loan?" Robert asked.

"I have discussed the banking options and believe I could arrange the capital provided I was careful. And, of course, if the purchase price did not exceed what I could borrow. Currently, there are only two on-going operations for sale, and they are of the size I would want, but I have not talked to either owner just yet. I plan to in the near future."

Robert turned to Brenda. "Tell me more about your greenhouse plans."

"My idea might only be a dream. The startup costs are high, and it could take a long time to make a profit."

"How so?"

"As a new business, I would need to build connections with the retailers that would be my largest customer base. The second hurdle is to identify the location and build new. That includes land, providing the zoning will allow." She gave Sheldon a smile. "I must work out each of these issues and then become an effective greenhouse owner."

***

Within a month, Sheldon learned of the possibility of purchasing an on-going operation near Hutchinson, Kansas. He and Brenda made an appointment with the owner, Mr. Henderson, and drove to the site. It was hard not to be excited about the possibility of relocating to the Hutchinson area, yet they wanted to be prudent in their first attempt to become business owners.

As they drove into the driveway, both Sheldon and Brenda were physically shaking from anticipation. Mr. Henderson greeted them at the front door and asked if they would like a cup of coffee. As they began to discuss the specifics of the sale, Mr. Henderson informed his guests that his wife had passed on, and that was the reason for the sale. He was anxious to reach an agreement.

"Would you like a tour of the house and breeding operation?" he asked. "We can take the Jeep out over the hundred and sixty acres after that."

They found the house in great condition—four bedrooms, a den, living room, kitchen with separate dining room, and a two-car garage.

The breeding operation included four registered Black Angus bulls complete with breeding pens, separate holding pens with water and feed troughs for the bulls, and safety equipment in each pen. There were twenty-five acres of land dedicated to breeding and was currently planted with grass and some flowers.

Some of the farm land had been leased to a Mr. Evens and converted to a lawn-growing operation. Evans wanted to continue the agreement for which he paid $7,500 per year.

"I can have a contract drawn up for $225,000 once your credit is approved," Mr. Henderson told them. "I'd need $35,000 down and $20,000 annually. I'd be willing to forego interest for the first fifteen years, but then we'd need to renegotiate terms after that."

Sheldon looked cautiously at Brenda. "How long until you need an answer?"

Mr. Henderson replied, "I'd take an earnest check for $10,000 which would go toward the down payment. Beyond that, I'll give you a week to decide."

Sheldon and Brenda were concerned with the down payment, but that was their only worry. Sheldon called his mother and explained to her the operation and the cost.

"Can I call you back within an hour?" Ellen asked.

"Yes. Please."

Ellen called Robert and explained Sheldon's opportunity.

"Do you think Sheldon and Brenda are up for the task?" he asked.

"I do. He's a very conscientious young man, and I think he will do well with the operation."

After some discussion, she called Sheldon back and explained that she could offer twenty thousand, and Robert had agreed to match it.

Sheldon called Mr. Henderson and agreed to meet his terms. "Sir, you have sold your farm! When would you like to close?"

"How about two weeks? I'm moving to Florida," Henderson said. "You are free to visit the farm and take inventory of anything in the house and garage that you might want. I'm not interested in paying to move all that stuff to Florida."

Brenda promised she would let Mr. Henderson know of anything she might want to keep.

After closing, Henderson called and informed her that she and Sheldon were free to occupy the house whenever they desired. When moving day arrived, she was excited to see that the kitchen was untouched by the packing company. This included a kitchen table and chairs that were very nice.

***

As the months passed, the Blakely family began to operate the Blakely Black Angus Breeding Operation. Sheldon's entire breeding stock consisted of four Black Angus bulls. He determined that he needed to advertise for potential customers beyond those already familiar with Henderson's operation. He consulted a marketing firm which payed a good dividend when seven customers called for delivery of Black Angus sperm. Within a month Sheldon began to think of hiring someone to assist him.

Over late-night dinners with Brenda, Sheldon discussed expanding his breeding operation to include Hereford and possibly Brahman or Charolais. He referenced several industry magazines that highlighted the popularity among beef producers and their customers.

"Why expand when you are just getting started with Black Angus?" Brenda asked.

"It's a matter of becoming *known* among beef producers and the veterinarians that serve them. While I do not intend to rush into something, I do want to discuss the potential and get your view."

Brenda looked worried and then said, "While we are discussing potential, there is sufficient land on this farm to build a greenhouse. Before we invest in expanding the cattle breeding program, I could use that money to live out a dream."

Sheldon smiled at his new wife. "You are correct. So how about you and I deciding where you want it, and we will stake it out."

Brenda was surprised at his response, but she was anxious to walk over the location she had in mind.

When she showed the plot to Sheldon, he began staking it out and then asked, "How large do you want the greenhouse?"

"I don't know yet. I'll have to research the matter and get back to you. Give me a couple of weeks."

A few days later, Brenda drove into Hutchinson and visited two retail greenhouses that were seasonal, and she learned that business was spotty. During one discussion, she found an employee Ken to be interesting and knowledgeable. After their discussion, Ken invited her for a cup of coffee and further discussion about her planned greenhouse. Coffee became dinner, and they learned that they had much in common. Toward the end of the meal, Brenda invited him to the farm.

The next day, Ken arrived at the Blakely Angus operation. Sheldon was going to be busy all day with the cattle, so Brenda took her guest to the plot where she wanted to locate the greenhouse.

"I was thinking of at least an acre of open field, but I'm not sure on the size of the greenhouse yet."

"I think you should go larger," Ken said. "Especially if you are wanting to supply several of the retail stores in the area."

She agreed readily, and they walked across the planned location, talking about possible plant species and what they would require. At one point, Brenda stumbled on a rough piece of ground and almost fell when Ken caught her and helped her regain her balance.

When they returned to the house, Ken said, "You really are a beautiful woman."

Brenda blushed and found she did not have a response.

"Can I take you to dinner again tonight?"

She reminded Ken that she was a married woman.

"And I'm a married man. That makes us even. But we can still enjoy dinner."

Brenda agreed, and they had an enjoyable evening.

***

The next week, after a trip for groceries, Sheldon and Brenda drove into the driveway leading to their new home. Brenda noticed a familiar car parked adjacent to the area she and Ken had walked the week before. When Ken got out of his car and started walking toward them, Brenda decided it was time to introduce the two men.

"Sheldon, this is Ken with Bowen's Greenhouse."

Ken offered his hand, but when Sheldon did not take it, he turned to Brenda. "It is good seeing you again. I was thinking about the greenhouse you discussed, and I began to wonder about zoning. I thought I would mention it so that detail can be taken care of before you get down the process and it might complicate matters."

"We'll look into," Sheldon said, abruptly. "Nice to meet you." He took Brenda's hand and pulled her toward the house.

Looking back, Brenda apologized for Sheldon, but that did not go over well. Embarrassed, she followed her husband into the house.

"Explain yourself!" she said to Sheldon when the door closed behind them.

Sheldon looked angry. "I will after you explain where you were after the greenhouses were closed.

"You were busy! Ken invited me to dinner, and I accepted. We talked about greenhouse operations, and he drove to the farm where I asked him about the site I had picked out. We walked across the area I planned for a greenhouse. Afterwards he left, and I walked into the house. Now, what else do you want to know?"

Sheldon's shoulders slumped. "Nothing else," he said, wondering if he could trust her. Was he being overly jealous? She had never before given him a reason to question her faithfulness, so he apologized for his outburst.

"I love you," Brenda said. "Remember that."

With their argument behind them, Sheldon turned his attention back to the breeding operation. He conferred with numerous veterinarians and discussed the need for artificial breeding of beef cattle, particularly Black Angus, Hereford and possibly Brahman or Charolais. He picked up several industry magazines pertaining to artificial breeding in Kansas, Oklahoma and Minnesota. He was surprised at the number of customers in Minnesota and planned to attend the Minnesota Veterinarians Association Annual meeting scheduled in St. Paul.

"I'll make reservations for us in St. Paul," Sheldon said one evening.

Brenda shook her head. "You should go alone. I'm so busy researching the greenhouse and need to get my ducks in a row before creating a financial plan." Weighing the options open to her, she looked over the papers she'd laid on the dining room table and then said, "It might be more productive to work for someone first. Get my feet wet before building a greenhouse of my own."

"This is your dream," Sheldon said.

"I know. But I'll have more details worked out by the time you return from Minnesota. When will you be back?"

"Saturday. Late." He thought it over and then said, "It might be Sunday if the conference runs long on Saturday."

Brenda found a resident expert on greenhouses and enlisted his help when contacting an architect. Albert handled much of the technical part of the discussion. Brenda, Albert and the architect agreed to meet at the chosen site and to go over her plans. The discussion was fruitful, and Brenda learned she had some decisions to make that would dictate the cost of the structure. The architect recommended a building that was about 150 feet wide and 300 feet long with a double deck at the eastern end that would serve as an office area while the remainder of the building would be dedicated to greenhouse activities. Brenda asked for rough sketches of their collective ideas and a copy of their notes to give to Sheldon.

After the two left, Brenda looked over the papers and decided to contact Ken for advice.

"How about I come over and look at the sketches?" Ken asked. "I can be there in thirty minutes."

When he arrived, he and Brenda walked across the site and discussed the building as sketched by the architect. Back at the house, Brenda offered Ken a glass of wine or coffee. He opted for the coffee as he was returning to work.

The next week, Sheldon and Brenda enjoyed sharing their respective research into cattle breeding and greenhouses. Brenda showed her husband the sketch prepared by the architect and quoted several statistics regarding specific plants to produce and those to avoid.

"How about we discuss this more over dinner," Sheldon said.

Brenda recommended her favorite restaurant, and Sheldon agreed.

In the middle of their meal, Brenda asked the breeding operation was shaping up.

Sheldon's eyes lit up. "I have an order for next week consisting of eight specimens to be delivered to a veterinarian in Stillwater, Oklahoma. Would you like to ride along?"

"Oklahoma. That's quite a ways. Are you planning on spending the night?"

"No," Sheldon said. "It will be a long one-day trip down and back."

Brenda wanted to support her husband, but she had plans of her own. "I'm not up for such a long drive in one day," she said.

Sheldon looked disappointed, but then he smiled at her. "I will have to leave early in the morning, and I know you're not a morning person." He looked down at the sketch of the building Brenda was considering and asked if she had received an estimate.

"Not yet. I'm waiting for the architect to recommend a particular siding and roofing material, and to finish design of the driveway."

As Brenda continued describing the issues with the greenhouse, Sheldon could not avoid thinking about his own projects—expanding his breeding operation and searching for two more registered bulls with an excellent bloodline.

The two finished dinner and headed back home.

In the morning, Sheldon left for Stillwater to make contact with the owner of two bulls that had the perfect heritage. He drove to their location and loaded one bull in his truck and brought him home. He went back later to load a three-year-old Brahman bull.

Along with the cattle, he obtained several documents describing their bloodlines and histories. Unloading each of the bulls was an exciting experience, and he asked Brenda to accompany him to view their latest purchase. While the two of them were overlooking the entire group of bulls, Sheldon indicated he needed to get an advertisement in the industry magazines that he was open for business. Brenda offered to write the ad for his review.

As the weeks passed, veterinarians became aware of the capability offered by the now named Midwest Artificial Insemination, LLC which stated the availability of registered Black Angus, Brahman and Charolais sires. *Call your veterinarian and schedule an appointment.* Within three days, Sheldon began receiving inquiries from veterinarians in Oklahoma, Kansas and Minnesota. Within the week, he had confirmed orders for sperm from each of the bulls, and he had to rush the orders. Within two weeks, he realized he would need an assistant.

Sheldon discussed hiring one person, and Brenda suggested the neighbor lady who lived one mile west of their home.

"Her name is Claudia," Brenda said, "and she has experience dealing with cattle."

When Claudia arrived for an interview, she answered Sheldon's questions knowledgeably. Her own husband worked six days a week, and that left little time for the two of them, so she would be available full time. They agreed she would start work on Monday of the next week.

Sheldon explained that the three bulls were different. The Angus was rather tame, and the Charolais was similar, but the Brahman warranted care as he was sometimes sensitive and could be dangerous.

"I've worked around difficult animals before," Claudia said, "and I will be careful. I know how to use a shock gun."

Sheldon monitored Claudia's work and was satisfied with everything she did. He complimented her on the manner in which she worked with the animals.

***

Sheldon reviewed mail from the Minneapolis Veterinarian Association to visit them and to explain how he was going to serve the bulls he advertised. When he called them, they asked him to visit them the following week and be prepared to tour their facilities and attend a meeting again in St. Paul. He agreed and left early the next morning. The discussions were shorter than he expected, so he returned early the next day.

The trip to Minneapolis produced enough orders for sperm deliveries to keep he and Claudia busy for three months. Additionally, Brenda informed him he had received several orders in the mail to be delivered to Stillwater, Oklahoma. Sheldon knew this would establish him in the business and discussed this with Claudia.

Brenda was busy with the design of the greenhouse and seemed excited about the prospects for success. She welcomed her mother, Caroline, who had come to visit for a week, and showed her both the greenhouse plans and Sheldon's operation.

"Where is all this money coming from?" her mother asked.

"It was from Sheldon's mom and dad."

Her mother was silent for a moment. "You do have the trust money from your father."

Brenda looked surprised. "I don't have access to that until I'm thirty."

"You don't have access on your own," Caroline agreed, "but I am the legal guardian of the funds. I could make it happen."

"Really? How much are we talking about?"

Her mother smiled slightly. "The fund is currently worth nearly one hundred thousand. For this project, as much as you've researched and organized, I could ask them to release the money early."

"Oh, Mother! Would you?"

They looked over the architectural drawing and walked across the site. As Brenda explained the interior of the building, she indicated where her office would be and estimated she would have two full time and one or two part time employees.

"I hope to be ready to start business by spring of next year."

They headed back to the house for coffee.

"This is a far cry from becoming a model," Brenda said.

"What? Why would you say that?" Caroline looked confused.

"That's what you wanted me to be, remember? You didn't think I needed a degree in anything. Just good looks."

Her mother looked a little embarrassed. "It was what my generation did," she said. "It was all we were expected to do. But it does seem like you and Sheldon have put a good thing together here. He's been very good for you."

Brenda blushed a little, unwilling to admit to her mother that not everything was good between her and her husband.

***

Sheldon was distracted by the sheer number of orders while trying to discuss the shipments to Stillwater. Claudia reminded him that she had already prepared those, and they were ready for shipment whichever way he wanted to handle the delivery.

"I think we need to set up a process to order online—streamlining everything, including the acknowledgments," he told her.

Claudia agreed and set to work.

After a couple of hours, Sheldon asked, "Are you overwhelmed with the events of the past week?"

"Not in the least," Claudia responded, her eyes sparkling with excitement. "I appreciate this job, and you."

The next week, Sheldon received a call from a Mr. Gilmore of Oklahoma City.

"I've been hearing good things about your artificial breeding and the sperm program. I'd like to know your availability and how soon I can get on the list."

"How many specimens would you like to order?"

"Well, I represent breeders all the way from Oklahoma City to the south and west to the Texas line. I estimated I would need more than one hundred orders—Black Angus and Charolais. That would be for the first month."

Sheldon tried to control his enthusiasm. "Thank you, Mr. Gilmore! Thank you very much. I'll make sure to deliver the goods promptly."

When he came into the house that evening, Brenda offered to show him the architect's drawing of her greenhouse.

"I'm sure it's great," Sheldon said. "But I have to eat and run. The operation is taking off in a hurry, and I am busy trying to catch up on these orders due soon."

"It will just take a minute," she insisted. "I have to give them my approval next week."

"Okay," Sheldon finally agreed as he grabbed leftovers from the fridge. "I will look at them tonight before I go to bed."

A couple of hours later, Sheldon came to bed and asked Brenda how she planned to finance her building.

"The cost estimate was more than I expected. I was intending to discuss this with the architect on Monday—hoping to eliminate a few things to lower the cost. Do you remember the trust money my father set up for me?"

Sheldon nodded.

"It's a hundred thousand dollars."

Sheldon let out a long sigh.

"I didn't think I had access to it for years yet, but Mom said she would make it happen."

"Really?"

"The architect quoted $135,000. I think I can get it down. Maybe my trust fund is all I would need."

"Maybe you go ahead, and we can finance the rest."

***

Brenda called the architect. "I am going to accept the design as offered. I would like to pay seventy-five thousand now and the remainder over the next year. Interest free, if that is acceptable to you."

The architect agreed, and they set a time to sign the paperwork.

Brenda called her mother to discuss getting the money from her trust fund.

"I'll contact the accountant," Caroline said. "Let me know when you need it. I am so excited about this project that I cannot think of anything else. This is amazing—my little girl doing such big things."

It gratified Brenda to know her mother was so supportive. "You should visit every so often to watch it go up."

"Would you mind?" Caroline asked.

"If I minded, I would not have suggested it. I will enjoy your company."

***

Brenda received the proceeds of her trust. When she transferred the funds, the banker asked if the greenhouse was a go.

"Yes," she said, smiling. "We are going to be a resounding success! Local nurseries will no longer need to order their supplies from a stranger as they will be able to walk in and pick their plants already for resale."

Sheldon and Claudia were busy with larger and larger orders from Oklahoma City asking for Black Angus, Brahman and Charolais. Sheldon began to research the capability of his bulls and found they can produce sperm daily for a short time, but the length of time depended on the quality of food each bull was consuming and the degree to which each bull digested the food. Sheldon contacted several veterinarians to get their view and discovered they did not know for sure.

He contacted Oklahoma State University. They suggested, for the optimum in pregnancy rates, it would be wise to use a bull for sperm collection on average, three times per week and not more than three ejaculations per day. The price per sperm donation was $18.00 as long as the bull has an excellent record of pregnancies. Sheldon would need to gather and keep records to support his claim of a high productive bull and advertise their success. This meant a lot to customers who gambled on their livestock to make them a profit.

Sheldon began to think of expanding his herd and contacted the gentleman who constructed his original bull pins—asking him to redesign the entire structure to accommodate another set of bulls equal to those he already had.

Sheldon asked Claudia what she thought about accommodating twice as many bulls as they had, and she asked how many hours Sheldon wanted her to work.

"I estimate we will both be busy full time, and there will be less travel as we will be needed at the breeding barn. Also, I need to streamline my bookkeeping system."

Brenda volunteered to revolutionize his bookkeeping methodology. She asked if he would like to have a web site highlighting his business.

"Yes, absolutely," he said.

Sheldon contacted the veterinarians with whom he did business and asked them if they had kept records of breeding successes and failures. About ninety percent responded with emails documenting the results of his bulls from the start to the last delivery. To date, his bulls had a positive record of more than ninety percent, and he was told he couldn't expect a better performance. He provided this information to Brenda who added the positive feedback to the web site. It told a good story about the success of Sheldon's bull breeding operation.

***

"Do you think it's time for us to have a baby?" Brenda asked one night.

"Only if we are committed to each other and no one else."

Brenda wondered what Sheldon already knew. "I have been thinking about the subject of unconditional love. It's a great goal, but it is not achievable."

"Not achievable? Do you really think that?"

Brenda shrugged. "We can try. I will commit myself to you provided you commit yourself to me."

"I thought I already had," Sheldon said.

The next morning, Sheldon got a cup of coffee and walked to the barn. Claudia was already on the job and progressing nicely to fill the orders that had arrived from Oklahoma City, Minneapolis and Kansas City. After assessing the amount of work needed to be done, he concluded they would be ready to ship all of them by noon Friday.

During a break, Claudia asked about her vacation time.

"What specifically do you want to know?"

"We have never discussed it, and I want to know when I can go on vacation and for how long. Do I get paid for it?"

Sheldon thought it over. "I've never had to consider this before, but how about one week paid at the end of the first year. Two weeks a year after that."

Claudia hugged Sheldon. "I've never had paid vacation before," she said when she pulled away. "Only one thing. I will miss our time together when I'm away."

Sheldon looked around to see if anyone else had overheard. "We can't keep seeing each other," he said. "It's time we end this affair."

Claudia looked devastated at first, but she nodded slightly. "I understand."

Sheldon departed to deliver the sperm specimens and spent time with the veterinarian customers with whom he had established effective customer relationships. While he was in between customers, he spent valuable time calculating ways to increase the number of sales. Returning home, he found several positive comments on the website.

Brenda was pleased to see him and welcomed him warmly. She wanted to talk about a number of subjects, namely the plans for their new wholesale greenhouse and the payment schedule she had established with the architect.

"What's your priority?" he asked.

"The greenhouse payment schedule," she replied. She gave Sheldon a brief rundown of the payment she had agreed to. "That leaves me with a balance of twenty-five thousand, but I'm asking you to pay the balance of twenty."

"The way things are going with the breeding program, I can do that," he replied. "Let me know when you need it."

Sheldon returned to his barn where the bull breeding operation was going full speed and found Claudia working as fast as she could. When she could take a break, she fell into Sheldon's arms and began to cry.

"My husband is moving us to Florida," she said.

"Do you want to go?"

Claudia shook her head. "Of course not."

A week passed. Sheldon walked over his farm trying to decide his next move. The one action he wanted to take was to purchase Claudia's farm if he could afford it. When he asked her how much her husband wanted, the price was twenty-five thousand less than he was expecting.

"I will buy it!" he blurted before he could collect himself.

When he walked into the house to tell Brenda the news, she met him with a stern look.

"I want a divorce," his wife said. "I'm moving out."

Blindsided, Sheldon tried to understand his feelings. He grieved over her decision, but he also felt a small measure of relief. It was not the end of the world. He would recover.

"What are we going to do about the greenhouse?" he asked.

Brenda looked at him scornfully. "I don't care," she said before walking away.

***

Two weeks later, someone knocked on Sheldon's door. He opened it to a beautiful lady standing on his front porch.

"Hi. I'm Juanita Barkley. Are you the gentleman who purchased Claudia and her husband's farm?"

"Yes!" He composed himself and asked her in. "Would you like a cup of coffee?"

When she said yes, he poured one for his guest and one for himself, but was so flustered by her beauty, he forgot to offer cream or sugar.

"I'll get to the point," she said. "My father died recently, and he left me a large sum of money. I was interested in purchasing the farm adjacent to mine on the east. I believe that's the one you just bought."

Sheldon gave Juanita a tour of his business, though she had already learned a great deal from Claudia.

"Who helps you with the bulls?" Juanita asked when they were in the barn.

"I'm actually looking for help now that Claudia has moved."

Juanita looked over the operation. "You know, I'm familiar with the animals, especially those wanting what the females have to offer."

Sheldon eyed her curiously. "Does that included those present?"

"Those currently present are excluded," Juanita quickly said.

Sheldon could tell his curiosity was creating an uncomfortable tension, so he asked to learn more about Juanita's education.

"I went to Stanford University," she said.

Sheldon thought of Brenda. "What was your major?"

"I got a masters degree in Animal Husbandry in 2105. That was the year my father died. That's when I started taking care of the farm."

"Would you like to discuss this more over dinner?"

Juanita accepted, and they spent a long evening drinking wine and talking into the night.

Early the next morning, Juanita called. "I know we had a lot to drink, but did you ask me to marry you last night?"

"I think so," Sheldon confirmed. "Was it weird?"

"Not really," she said. "How about you come to breakfast and we discuss it some more."

They enjoyed a nice breakfast and exchanged stories of their histories including the good and not so good parts of Stanford and the University of Illinois. Juanita could tell that Sheldon became depressed every time she mentioned Illinois. She assumed it was because of his recent divorce.

At one point, Sheldon asked, "When did you relocate to the farm?"

"In February after my Father died. I have been on the farm for five months, and I love it except for the lack of money. Everything I inherited is tied up in legal issues, but that will be over in another month."

Sheldon opened his wallet. "Will five hundred hold you over?" Juanita started to turn him down, but he insisted.

***

Sheldon and Juanita's families attended the wedding on March seventh. Juanita's family was pleased to be associated with the agricultural effort and a person so dedicated to Juanita. Sheldon's family was more than concerned about the fact that Sheldon's divorce had been finalized only two days earlier.

A month later, Sheldon was busy tending to the bulls and shipments of sperm. He was expecting Juanita's return from a previously scheduled appointment with her physician and a second appointment with the banker to settle the paperwork on merging Juanita's farm and the one now owned by Sheldon and Juanita. The merger would result in property consisting of 480 acres of prime Kansas soil.

Sheldon heard a lady's voice call for him and, when he opened the door, Brenda started to enter. The two collided into the arms of the other.

"Oh! Hello," Sheldon said. They separated, and he asked, "What brings you back here?"

"I saw the ad in the paper for an administrative records position. I'm here to apply."

Sheldon eyed her curiously. "Are you sure that's a good idea?"

"You can test me if you like."

Sheldon tried to keep pace with the bulls as he discussed his requirements for the position and while simultaneously trying to assess what Brenda actually knew about the breeding end of the business.

Brenda held her ground and asked several questions which indicated she knew more than Sheldon thought she did.

"Can you demonstrate your expertise in handling a bull?"

She pulled it off deftly.

Sheldon was still uncertain, so he determined to find a weakness. None surfaced. And since Claudia had moved on, Sheldon was reluctant to pass on someone that knowledgeable.

"Okay," he finally agreed. "You are hired. When can you start?"

"Early Monday morning," she said, grinning. As she leaned in to give Sheldon a hug, Juanita entered the bull barn.

Walking up to them, Juanita frowned at her husband. "And who is this?"

"Juanita!" Sheldon backed away from his ex and took his new wife by the hand. Turning back to Brenda, he said, "This is my wife, Juanita. Juanita, this is Brenda."

"Brenda? The woman you just divorced?"

In the awkward few seconds that followed, Brenda shook her head. "Don't worry. I'm not here to reclaim him."

The three headed to the house so that the two women could become more acquainted, and Sheldon could explain why he had finally succumbed to Brenda's request for a job. At Juanita's urging, Brenda stayed for lunch, and the two women realized they actually liked one another.

After Brenda left, promising to return for work on Monday, Juanita pulled Sheldon aside. "You seriously think the two of you can work together? There still seems to be an obvious connection between you."

"She applied for the job, and I don't have anyone else as qualified."

Juanita shook her head. "This is not smart, Sheldon."

"I know," he said. "But Brenda is a smart woman. We'll make it work."

Juanita was concerned, but she tried to stay calm. She realized not just the potential for conflict between the three of them, but wondered if the situation would create controversy for Sheldon's clients if the situation became known.

Later that night, Sheldon raised the issue again.

"I know you're not comfortable with Brenda working here."

"I'm just concerned that the two of you will rekindle feelings for each other. And I'm aware of your histories. Neither one of you were monogamous while you were married. Of course, I'm going to be concerned."

"What can I do to assure you?" Sheldon asked.

"I don't know. But be sure of this. If I even suspect the two of you are having an affair, I will assert myself in a manner that will never be forgotten."

***

Several months into their marriage, a certified letter arrived. When Sheldon opened it, his eyes grew wide. "It's from my father, Robert Glasco. He's offering us an all-expense paid cruise to Morocco!"

Juanita read the letter. "They need to know in the next five days." She looked up at her husband. "The cruise is two weeks long. Is it possible for us to get away that long?"

"I can't think of any way to make that happen. Not with the business we have now."

Reluctantly, Sheldon called his father and explained the situation.

"Perhaps we could visit you when we return," he father suggested.

They made their plans, and the Mr. and Mrs. Glasco scheduled a flight on their return.

When the Glasco's arrived, Sheldon introduced them to his new wife.

"So nice to meet you," Ellen said, leaning in to hug her daughter-in-law.

When Juanita escorted her mother-in-law into the house, Sheldon took Robert to the barns.

"Business is booming," he said, showing Robert all of the breeding pens and the collecting operation. "I can hardly keep up." He added, "Also, the man leasing the acreage for the grass-growing operation is going to retire. Juanita and I are considering the expansion of that operation, as well. Currently we have approximately one hundred acres dedicated to this effort. We are discussing the expansion of this to two hundred and fifty acres, utilizing land Juanita inherited from her father. Perhaps you may want to do some research on this idea. I need all the help I can get as I am a beginner."

"So you think I'd like to grow grass," he father said, a twinkle in his eye.

"No need. The operation is already in place, for the most part. Grass is a cash crop and will be operated without our involvement except to cash the check annually."

"Doesn't that mean you can oversee it easily?"

"I won't have the time. I am expanding the number of bulls to increase the types of semen I plan to offer the community. Juanita and I have discussed this, and I am currently looking to purchase one Brahman, one Charolais and one Hereford bull. This effort will expand our operation considerably."

"What about the greenhouse?"

Sheldon shook his head. "Brenda turned in her two-week notice last week. We are looking for personnel again. Our advertisement is out for Brenda's replacement."

"You might want to slow down, son."

"I disagree," Sheldon said. "We need to strike while the iron is hot. We are considering additional ideas as to the artificial insemination business. I have discussed these with the professors at my old alma mater, the University of Illinois. They seem to be interested."

Sheldon met with Mr. Edelman who had constructed the current bull pens and asked him to design or redesign the layout of pens to allow the bulls to enter and depart the semen collection area to accommodate the new bulls without causing conflict.

Business happened fast. Three college students applied for the advertised positions, and Sheldon scheduled interviews the following week. All three were well qualified for the positions offered. At the same time, Claudia called from Florida and asked for her old job back.

"Wonderful!" Sheldon said when Juanita delivered the news. "Call her back and tell her yes. Immediately!" He was aware that his wife did not know Claudia was the one he'd had an affair with. He intended to keep his work relationship very professional this time around.

On the Monday that Claudia arrived for work, Representatives from Kansas State University came to assist Sheldon in his efforts. Juanita also contacted the college-age applicants and asked if they would agree to temporary positions to see how well they could adjust to the work.

"Claudia knows this operation inside and out," Sheldon told Juanita that morning. "What do you think of giving Claudia the position of manager?"

"If you think she can handle the herd of bulls, then I say yes."

Mr. Edelman completed the redesign of the bull pens three weeks later. Unfortunately, the feeders needed to be manually refilled to meet the requirement for each bull. It was heavy labor.

Sheldon and Juanita contracted with a trucker to bring home twelve new bulls. Meanwhile, they held a staff meeting to stress treatment of the bulls.

"You must never mistreat a bull," Sheldon insisted. "Always show respect for a bull. Most importantly, know that a bull can and will injure and kill a human if you are not practicing safe handling at all times. Remember, these bulls are huge, weighing a ton in most cases. And they can be quick and fast." He turned the floor over to Claudia.

"We will be discussing our total work effort," she began, "and conducting a thorough training program to ensure we work in a safe and productive manner. It will benefit all of us when we know our job and perform it safely. We will use this week to study, train and go through several practice runs with the bulls that will be delivered on Thursday.

"We will be adding to our current herd, and we will also stay abreast of available bulls that are produced by beef producers who periodically have more young stock than they want to retain. We will house these bulls on the "Juanita" farm until they are ready for service." She nodded at Sheldon's wife.

When she had finished her part of the meeting, Sheldon said, "We began this day with a new manager, Claudia, and three new sperm collectors—Ronald, Darrell, and Jeffrey. Claudia will start their training following a brief introduction and tour of the facilities. Juanita will be present to cover administrative requirements and leave policies."

That evening, Juanita approached Sheldon about starting a family.

"Are you pregnant?" Sheldon asked, a bit distracted with his thoughts.

"What if I was?"

Sheldon sat up and looked at his wife. "Are you?"

"No. I'm not. But I have to tell you, I've been patient for too long. It's time we made a plan, or at least a concerted effort."

Sheldon thought it over before taking his wife to bed.

***

Six months later, the periodic evaluations of the bull semen collection process was completed with the Angus and Hereford. Sheldon posted a memorandum about the nutritional requirements for the entire herd. The plans were to produce sixty donations per week from the herd. He wanted to stay a step ahead of the customers, but he also wanted to avoid collecting sperm for which there was no market.

"I'm seeking information from each of you concerning travel to meet and discuss several functions to keep the operation working smoothly. If you are interested, please let Claudia know. The priority for travel will normally be Sheldon, Claudia, Volunteer# 1, 2, and 3, based on a planned schedule."

When he found out Juanita was pregnant, Sheldon put plans for the greenhouse on hold.

Three months later, business had increased in the semen production area, lawn grass operations were producing as projected, and there were two customers who had agreed to partner on the greenhouse and open a wholesale business. At this point, Brenda asked to resign, and she agreed to take a sum relative to her investment in the greenhouse as her severance pay.

Sheldon enjoyed management of their real estate and associated businesses. Meanwhile, Juanita began to prepare their home for twins.

After completing a thorough review, Sheldon asked his parents to visit them and allow time for an in-depth discussion regarding the business. "And you can meet your new grandchildren."

Late one evening, Juanita approached Sheldon with a drink in hand and requested to talk about her plans for the future. "Have you ever given consideration to the total number of children you would like?"

"We already have a great start," Sheldon said. "How many do you want?"

"I would like to continue growing our family," Juanita said. "I also want to discuss an idea I had after my father died. Perhaps we should start raising young bulls."

"That is an excellent idea," Sheldon told her.

He talked with Claudia about advertising in Oklahoma, Nebraska, Minnesota, Kansas and Illinois and expanding the capabilities of the Midwest Artificial Insemination, LLC and the Evans Lawn and Grass LLC.

Sheldon's parents responded to the opportunity to visit their son and his family, and to become more familiar with the ever-increasing business activities that has become exceedingly successful. While Robert was curious about the artificial breeding operation, Sheldon's mother had informed him she wanted to spend time with Juanita and to become more familiar with her daughter-in-law and grandsons. After letting their guests relax and catch up on the latest news about the business, Juanita informed Sheldon's parents they were going to be grandparents again.

"I'm so excited for you!" Ellen said, hugging the young couple.

"Twins again?" Robert asked.

Juanita smiled at Sheldon. "Wouldn't that be nice? Get it over with all at once, but no. We're only having one."

They talked over due dates and the fact that the couple wanted a girl this time.

After dinner, Robert and Ellen were surprised to learn that Juanita and Sheldon owned a very large number of acres at this point. Their latest purchase was agreed to in a ten-minute discussion between the seller and Juanita causing Sheldon to declare her a true and progressive capitalist.

"Are you through buying land?" Robert asked Sheldon.

"We are through purchasing land until we get a chance to buy more," he said. "We would like to own this entire section if the price is right."

"What about the lawn business?"

Sheldon and Juanita exchanged glances.

"It's expanding at a rapid rate. We had planned to make some adjustments, but Brenda is negotiating with the current owners. She would like to buy it, if we agree. This is something we need to discuss."

"It would be nice to assist Brenda," Ellen said. "You go back a long time, and she was responsible for the architectural design of the greenhouse."

Sheldon nodded. "Also, Brenda wants to be in the greenhouse business again. She has been here looking at the operation, and she is aware that Mr. Evans is not in good health. He has hinted at selling his interests to Brenda."

Ellen looked at Juanita. "Could you live with Brenda being the owner?"

"It would complicate business matters," Sheldon admitted.

"I'm not talking about business matters," his mother said.

Juanita lowered her eyes to the floor. "I don't like the idea," she said. "I know Sheldon is still in love with her."

Sheldon shook his head. "Mr. Evans is in love with Brenda. He wants to marry her."

"That's not an answer," Ellen said. "Juanita is right. I can see you still have feelings for your first wife."

"It's more than that," Juanita told her in-laws. "Brenda wants Sheldon back. And I'm inclined to let her have him."

This shocked everyone in the room, especially Sheldon.

"I asked the two of you here because I needed a buffer between me Sheldon when I asked for a divorce."

"A divorce?" Robert gave his son a questioning look.

Juanita continued. "I have plans to return to California with my children. I want to sell my interest in the farm. My life here has been hard work, no vacation, and it has been boring. My husband works all the time and has no future but to work. When we make ten cents we purchase another farm and work to pay for the farm." She wrung her hands. "Before my father died, farm life was great, but no more. It is not for me."

Sheldon was speechless. He could not fathom losing the wife he loved and being separated from his children.

Ellen looked sympathetically at her daughter-in-law. "I can't say that I'm surprised, though this does seem sudden."

"Not sudden for me," Juanita told her. "I've been trying to get my husband's attention for years now. But he's always more interested in talking with Brenda or Claudia or even the cows."

Everyone was silent for a few moments.

At last, Juanita said, "When I get my portion of the business, I will put a percentage in trust for the children's future. I won't need the money. I have a long-time friend who has been courting me for years. He's independently wealthy. I think I deserve to be taken care of for a change."

Sheldon looked angry. "And what if I decide that I want custody of the children?"

Juanita's eyes widened. "Seriously? You hardly spend time with them as it is!" The thought brought tears to her eyes.

Robert held up his hand. "I think we need to calm down, and perhaps we all need a good night's sleep before discussing this any further."

When the phone rang, Sheldon walked into another room to answer it. The Minneapolis Cattlemen's Association and Veterinarians were asking him to participate in the conference as a speaker for one of the breeding workshops. He told them he would have to call them back.

When he walked back into the living room, he looked haggard. "I'm needed in the barn," he said, making his apologies. He did not tell them that he also needed time to think.

***

Sheldon walked out across the land he owned. On his return to a vacant house, he was struck by the emptiness that once was busy with little feet. The quiet only frustrated him more, so he wandered to the barn where he found Ronald and Jeffrey busy with the production of semen and filling orders. There, he encountered Brenda.

"Are you still interested in making a deal on the greenhouse?" she asked. "I'm sorry," she said before he could answer. "It seems like a rotten day to make a deal."

Sheldon managed a smile and invited Brenda to the house for a drink.

"What's wrong?" she asked once they were seated in the living room.

Sheldon showed her the letter he had received from Juanita about the divorce.

"Oh! I didn't know. Are you okay?"

They talked about life for a while—filling in the time they were apart.

"There was no life for me without you," Brenda said. "There was no fondness, nor tenderness. No warmth, no devotion, no adoration. No life."

"I didn't know," he said. "I thought you were happy."

"I made a promise not to interfere with your marriage. I couldn't tell you how I really felt." She looked him in the eyes. "Would you want to live together again?"

Sheldon looked at her for a long time. "You could never share yourself with another man again. Not while you're committed to me."

The next week, Brenda stopped in to say that she was going to move out of her rented apartment and move her belongings to the house.

"I'm glad," Sheldon said. "It seems that we have a chance to correct a serious mistake. Now, perhaps, we will learn from this mistake."

He took Brenda's hand and led her to the bedroom.

[]Afterward, Sheldon left Brenda and returned to the barn. It felt good to be able to relax while doing something he loved. Brenda seemed to understand that better than Juanita ever had.

"You look happy," Claudia said when she saw him. "Is Brenda really moving back in?"

"Yes," Sheldon told her.

She eyed him curiously and then asked, "Are you free to make time for me again?"

"Not now. I must be good."

Claudia looked mildly disappointed. "I understand," was all she said and returned to processing semen from the bulls.

When she saw Brenda again, she asked if Sheldon was different now than before their separation.

"Yes, he is much different," she said. "He misses his children. One other difference, I am not certain of his love for me like it was before we split. I do not think he trusts me as he did when we were first married. Of course, I deserve that."

Brenda prepared dinner for the two of them and, afterwards, asked Sheldon if it would be okay if she could be instated as the manager of the greenhouse operation. "I wans the authority to manage it the way I think it should be managed."

"I need to discuss it with Mr. Evans," he told her. "He wants out of his arrangement with you, and I think he will agree."

Several weeks passed, and Brenda informed Sheldon that Mr. Evans was ill and wanted to talk. Sheldon went to visit him at the greenhouse office.

"I want to give Brenda my interest in the operation. My doctor told me to divest myself of any assets I no longer wanted." He shifted in his chair. "I don't have long to live."

Sheldon frowned.

"Cancer. Can you prepare the paper work that would make it official?"

"I will do whatever you need," Sheldon said. "I can get it started today, if you like."

When Sheldon informed Brenda, she cried like a baby and prayed for Mr. Evans.[]

"Is there anything I can do for you?" he asked.

Brenda wrapped her arms around him and said, "Perhaps we should get married again."

***

The greenhouse operation was going well with Brenda as the new manager. Life on the farm seemed to be getting back to that idyllic time when Sheldon and her were first married. One evening, following a busy week, Brenda informed Sheldon that she wanted to start a family.

"It's time you and I got serious about our original plans."

"I do have an artificial insemination business," Sheldon joked. "Perhaps we take advantage of that."

"Only for the income it provides," Brenda insisted. But she smiled at his sense of humor.

"There is enough income to pay for several increases in the family structure, so please let me know when we must stop or when we get to fifteen. Whichever comes first."

Brenda forced a smile but wondered if he was serious. Was he really thinking of fifteen?

Being in a romantic mood, he stood toe to toe with Brenda and noticed tears pooling in the corners of her eyes. He wrapped his arms around her and said, "Honey, you and I must let the ugly past we caused be still. Let God take care of that part of us, and let the good part of our hearts and souls live in Jesus our Savior."

"Remember our college days and think of us as we were—clean, in love with each other, not allowing bad stuff in our minds. It was chemistry. Our prayers to Jesus Christ lifted us up, and we would smile knowing God was with us."

"We are together again," he said, "so hopefully God will guide both of us."

They held each other tight, and Brenda whispered, "Jesus be with Sheldon and me in this

time of need."

***

Sheldon walked to the barn and talked with Claudia, Ron, Darrel and Jeffrey. He joked with each employee, making small talk and enjoying his renewed relationship with his staff. A few moments later, Brenda approached the crew and handed each one a cookie she had just taken out of the oven. She then turned to Sheldon and gave him a kiss.

"My cookie is better than your cookie," he joked.

They commented, "Oh sure."

When Sheldon returned to the house for lunch, Brenda informed him she was ready to brief him on the latest shipments of semen.

"Speaking of semen," she said, "there is one more thing. We have a little one on the way."

Sheldon raised an eyebrow. "Who's the father?"

Brenda boxed him on the shoulder. "You seriously have to ask?"

He smiled as he remembered back to their college life. He and Brenda had made many mistakes in their relationships. Perhaps he had gotten into the artificial insemination business a little too quickly. It had certainly put a strain on their marriage the first time. But this time, the two of them had made a decision to focus on improving the quality of life with each other, raise their family in a loving and caring relationship and to let Jesus Christ lead them.

"Can I bring up a sensitive subject that embarrasses me? I'm a little afraid."

"Be brave, and trust Jesus," he said. "Go ahead."

"At a bad time in my life, I profaned myself, you, and Jesus Christ. But I promise to not ever do it again."

"You were not the only one," he admitted. Neither of us can claim to be innocent."

"But I dream of doing it again," Brenda admitted. "Can you help me avoid the pitfalls that led to such behavior?"

"I can certainly try," Sheldon said, and they talked about it for hours.

"I love you," his wife said before they went to bed.

"And I you," he responded. "Tonight, we just dream of each other."

To Serve the Young

The rain kept falling, washing away tears from Susan's eyes. She knew her father was watching, but she kept walking. She was determined to leave the man who was obsessed with earning money, saving money, investing money, and building a fortune for no apparent reason. They already had money. The family assets were in the millions.

Susan liked the attention her father gave her—most of the time. But lately, he constantly wanted to direct her toward certain educational pursuits that she had no interest in. Her father's obsession was driving a wedge between them. She was determined to leave home at the early age of seventeen. A beautiful girl with long, blond hair, bluish-green eyes and a smile that captivated even a casual acquaintance, she believed she could make her own way in the world.

This desire for independence had been brewing for a long time. As young as eight years old, she had discussed this matter with a school counselor and the church pastor. She asked for advice from both of them—thought to be trusted friends—and they gave her the same answer. "Discuss this with your father." She took their advice, but the only thing her father would discuss was economics, earning and saving money, and how to be obedient to the wishes of her father. Because they were never close, she seldom had discussions with her mother.

On this early morning in June, Susan decided the time was right. She walked down the long driveway of her family's ten-acre estate and wept at the thought of missing her father. She assumed he would come after her, do something to stop her as she was "daddy's little girl." When he didn't, she began to question her judgment and her determination. She had tried to leave twice before and failed, but not this time. She was too proud to let him win again.

As Carl watched his daughter leave, he began to pray out loud. "Father in Heaven I place Susan in your hands, please protect her. As talented as she is, she needs you. She is naïve." He watched as she boarded a bus at the corner.

Angry, he immediately canceled her cell phone. "This will create an immediate sense of urgency," he thought. "She will have to learn the hard way."

As the bus moved down the street, Carl wiped tears from his eyes. Returning to his study, he made note of his daughter's departure in his diary and wrote the prayer he had prayed.

Martha entered the study. "Is she gone," Susan's mother asked.

Carl stared sullenly into the distance. After a few moments, Martha took his silence as confirmation and left the study.

Martha considered Susan her most difficult child—complex, vivacious and more confident than Martha had ever been, even as an adult. Her youngest daughter demonstrated eccentricities that few of her family or closest friends understood.

Susan's pursuit of educational opportunities was unusually rare, and neither her mother nor her father could relate to the girl's progressive stance on world issues. She spent hours studying the humanities, dancing, religion, science and five different languages. She embarked on her journey to become educated while she was very young—too young according to her father who thought her too impressionable.

When Susan had turned seventeen, her father, mother and sister attended the Kennedy Center for the Performing Arts. She enjoyed everything she observed or heard. Her beauty and infectious smile captured the attention of many. Toward late evening, Susan was approached by Cassidy Wilcox, a Wyoming bronc buster cowboy who seldom lost at anything. For this occasion he was planning his own social hour and asked if she would join him. Susan politely informed him that she had scheduled a prior engagement. Cassidy was persistent, however, and asked to exchange phone numbers.

The Kennedy Center social hour involved dancing, conversation, and great food. Susan had little chance to advance her own agenda. She returned to the hotel with her family and decided to relax with a massage and restful sleep.

At breakfast the next morning, Susan received a personal call from Mr. Wilcox requesting that she accompany him to a football game between the New York Mets and the Washington Redskins. Susan tried to refuse.

"I'm flying home to Portland, Oregon with my family in the morning."

"That shouldn't be a problem," Cassidy said. "I have my own jet. Spend the night with me, and I can fly you home myself."

"I don't think so," Susan told him. "I'm only seventeen. I'm sure my parents would not approve."

"Seventeen!" He looked surprised and then gave her a wink. "I thought you were older."

When Susan told her father about Cassidy's advances, she made it clear she was not tempted. Even so, her decision to turn Cassidy down weighed on her mind, especially when she found herself needing to defend her integrity. A part of her liked the attention, and she asked herself how she could play it to her advantage.

She asked her mother one day if it was normal for men to pursue a girl so young.

"Unfortunately, yes," Martha said. Her mother avoided a lengthy answer—afraid Susan would inquire further into her own activities when she was even younger than her daughter. She was not a model parent.

Susan then asked her father if all men pursued young women for the purpose of personal enjoyment. His response was, "Who else would they pursue?"

***

Susan's mother was a very private person, never revealing her inner self even to Susan's father who was a well-known Certified Public Accountant, senior partner in his law firm, and was a member of the Board of Seniors who advised the firm on controversial matters. The only person who knew Martha better than Carl was her lover, Alfred.

Martha and Alfred had a long-standing intimate relationship that provided her with the love missing from her marriage. Carl was a busy man thereby allowing ample time for his wife to do as she pleased. Martha suspected Susan knew too much about her affair, yet Susan always kept whatever she knew to herself. Her mother managed to rendezvous with Alfred monthly, but if she needed something more urgent, Alfred was quick to respond.

Susan, on the other hand, was not interested in relationships with boys in high school. She concentrated on her studies and completed high school in two years with a 4.0 GPA. She had also taken a number of college-level courses. While her mother explored the cadre of colleges and universities, Susan narrowed down her criteria.

Susan decided on the University of Notre Dame in South Bend, Indiana. Her mother was angry and said so.

"But Mother," Susan said sarcastically, "there are more virile men at Notre Dame than anywhere else."

When Susan met with the university counselors, they were in disbelief of her transcripts from high school.

One of the counselors turned to her and said, "Your transcripts reflect completed college level credits sufficient to place you as a third-year student. We have never done that, however, if we do not, you may be required to retake some courses in which you have already earned an A."

Susan looked disappointed. "What can you do to make this happen?"

"We would normally ask that you pay a minimum for the credits already attained at this level, and there will be the additional costs of remaining credit hours plus housing."

"Do you require this of your star football players?"

"Well, no," the counselor said, looking a bit dismayed.

"I think it's only fair to be treated equally."

Moments later, Susan completed her enrollment with all costs—including room and board—paid by the university.

She was a model student and became engaged in numerous activities associated with pediatric medicine and the study of vaccines in children. She also asked to be included in studies sponsored by the Mayo Clinic dealing with the same subject.

Susan quickly discovered that the mannerisms and interests of the men in pediatric medicine were directed at research and not at relationships with women. She began to explore other areas for social connection with men. Cassidy Wilcox's name surfaced, and Susan called him. They talked for a long time and promised each other to stay in touch.

The discussions with members of the Mayo Clinic were interesting and informative. She found significant challenges that interested her beyond the classroom. One specific challenge was a beautiful young girl with long curly, blonde hair who doctors had not been successful in diagnosing. Her name was Judith Ann, ten years of age, with parents who did not have the financial means to always be present when Judith needed them.

Susan fell in love with Judith and began an in-depth study of her condition. During data recording and analysis, Susan began to notice information similar to a patient she had studied in high school. The patient, Caroline, was a ten-year young child in the Congo. She displayed behavioral traits similar to that displayed by Judith. The disease was thought to be Kaposi's sarcoma due to its cancer orientation beginning at a young age. Susan coordinated with the Mayo Clinic and arranged to travel to the Congo with Judith to study the two girls. Within a few weeks, Susan and the study group had isolated identical data pertaining to the Congolese girl and Judith. In discussions with doctors in the Congo, they were able to isolate a small number of similar cases.

On the return trip, the clinic group mapped out a plan of attack to deal with Judith Ann. The group thanked Susan for her contributions. Returning to her studies, she had to play catch up, taking four examinations within a week. When the grades were posted, she smiled knowing she had another semester of As.

Taking a mental break, she called Cassidy, and they talked for several hours. She told him that she was extremely concerned about Caroline and Judith Ann. While they lived in countries far apart from each other, they shared the same misfortune of being diagnosed with an illness with no known cure. She explained to Cassidy that the Mayo Clinic had proposed they be granted permission to become foster parents to the two girls.

"They want me to be the person in charge of the girls. I'd be their parent, sister, counselor and buddy while simultaneously studying their illness."

"How do you feel about that?" Cassidy asked.

"Honestly, I'm thrilled. It's just a lot of responsibility."

***

When the time came, Susan met Caroline at the airport. She had planned a number of activities involving the two young ladies for the first month of their stay in South Bend. Susan had a light schedule as it was the close of one semester of school, and the second had yet to begin. She kept the two girls occupied with cooking, which they enjoyed. On Friday, she scheduled some activities for the girls to participate in and exercise their muscles. They attended the University of Notre Dame basketball game between Notre Dame and Michigan. The teams had been informed of the girls' condition, and one of the players pulled Caroline from her seat and carried her on his shoulder so she net a ball for two points. She was so excited, she wanted pictures of her achievement.

On Monday, the girls were subjected to several tests. The team prescribed a course of medicines that made the girls ill and had to be discontinued. With some fine-tuning, the new medicines worked fine with no adverse effects. Personnel from the clinic were impressed with the progress of both Caroline and Judith Ann and asked their guardians and the University of Notre Dame participants to consider a three-week study on site at the Rochester, Minnesota. The Mayo Clinic group proposed a no-cost study, on site, with several of their medical staff participating and a final report of their findings presented at the conclusion. Susan asked if she could be a major participant in finalizing the reports. She was assured she would be involved.

Susan asked the university for permission to take a break from her studies. She scheduled a three-day event to provide Caroline and Judith Ann an outing to interact with young lambs, goats, piglets and puppies. Additionally, they scheduled educational opportunities for the girls.

When they returned home, Caroline mentioned one of the guys assigned to handle the animals. "You should meet Brack," she told Susan.

"Brack?" Susan smiled at the young girl.

"Yes, he's really nice."

Susan let the subject drop.

Weeks later, the clinic called to coordinate the on-site study. Susan was excited to attend. When they were discussing clothes to pack, the girls did not have the items recommended. Susan offered to purchase the items needed as long as the Mayo Clinic reimbursed her.

"So, you girls want to go shopping?"

"Yes, yes, yes!"

They called for a taxi, and on the way to the mall, Caroline asked, "Susan, have you called the animal handler?"

"Who?"

"Brack. Can I use your phone to call him?"

"Do you know his number?"

Caroline smiled. "Yes. I liked Brack and asked for his number at the zoo." She punched in the number and, when Brack answered, they had a brief conversation.

"He was very nice and promised to call you," she said when she hung up. "I told him he shouldn't wait or some other guy was going to take advantage of you, and he would be out of luck."

***

Susan was aware of everyone demanding her time. At least it seemed that way. She needed time away from the stress, so she checked the weather in Puerto Vallarta. She inquired about available rentals for one week for a party of two. Susan called Cassidy and asked if he would join her.

"Yes, yes," he said. "When?"

"In three weeks?"

"I can manage that. I'll schedule a flight plan tomorrow. Should I bring anything special?"

"Just yourself," she said.

Making plans was not as easy as Susan had hoped. Caroline and Judith Ann expressed concern that she was leaving, even if for a short while. The girls missed their parents. Susan had become a surrogate, and that was a new feeling for her. She had never before enjoyed such a close relationship.

"I will be gone for a short week, and I will call periodically," she told the girls.

Susan and Cassidy made plans to meet at the university before flying to Mexico. Their week seemed to be the escape they had both hoped for.

When Susan returned, she dove into her work at the university, working hard to improve the lives of Caroline and Judith Ann. Regardless, she was concerned as she was carrying a heavy academic load and wanted to reserve sufficient time for her two girls. Additionally, her mother called to complain that Susan was neglecting her visits home, and she missed her.

"I promised, Mom. I will make a trip home next month."

Her mother inquired about the girls, wondering how much of it was consuming Susan's time.

"The girls are improving and maturing. It's important that they have someone stable in their lives at this point."

The results of the Mayo Clinic study had been determined and were going to be explained on Thursday and Friday of the following week. Susan wanted to be prepared for whatever surfaced. Caroline and Judith Ann seemed to be two happy girls growing every day. Susan could not think of anything that the study could mention that would be a surprise to her. She attended the briefing and was disappointed that nothing more had been determined.

"Do you intend to conduct further studies?"

"Not at this time."

The girls were disappointed that they would soon be returned to their families, and Susan would return to the pursuit of her doctorate in medical science. Susan coordinated with the guardians and invited the girls for dinner at the University of Notre Dame student union—Caroline and Judith Ann's place of choice. When it came time to order, both young ladies reviewed the menu, asking questions and ordering hamburgers and fries with a lot of "katsup." There was plenty of chatter between them, most of which was typical of ten-year young girls.

A friend of Susan's stopped by to chat about college, and they became engrossed in a conversation regarding medical terms contained in their upcoming examination.

While walking back to their rooms, Judith Ann asked Susan how old she was when she first made love with a man.

Shocked, Susan said, "That is a private matter between the two people who are in love with each other."

She turned the discussion to something harmless, but wondered if the girls were old enough for sex education. She did not feel particularly qualified because of her limited experience, and there was a huge difference in maturity between Caroline and Judith Ann. Susan decided to turn their curiosity toward a subject more personal to both of the girls, and she consulted with two instructors she knew in the field of child psychology.

After talking with them, both instructors agreed to participate in a round table the following Wednesday provided the young ladies would submit three questions to be answered. Susan had the girls work together. After some discussion, they settled on their questions. "Will we ever be free of skin issues? How deep does the skin become infected? Can we ever plan to be completely healed?" Susan read the questions and cried.

At Wednesday's round table, the discussion centered on cancer of the skin—primarily on treatment of soft tissue, radiation, surgery and chemotherapy with emphasis on quality care.

"Do you have answers for the girls?" Susan asked.

"Yes," one instructor stated, looking at the girls. "And we will be totally honest with you. As for your skin issues, you will probably deal with them for the rest of your lives." He could not bring himself to suggest that their lives might be very short.

A second instructor took up the next question. "The skin can become infected very deeply. Sometimes to the bone."

Both girls looked disheartened.

The third instructor saw their fear and quickly added, "One should never give up hope. Medicine is advancing every day."

***

Susan awakened on Saturday morning to the happy chatter of the two girls, and she proposed they go shopping for girl stuff. The outing took several hours because Caroline and Judith Ann tried on thirty-three pairs of shoes before selecting one pair each. The shoe salesman was sweating profusely. On the way home, Susan treated both to hamburgers, fries and a coke.

Late in the afternoon Susan received an urgent call from the lead person heading the Mayo Study Group and requested an emergency meeting without Caroline and Judith Ann present. The Mayo lead gave Susan the bad news.

"We've discovered cancer cells in the lungs and liver of both Caroline and Judith Ann."

After Susan had recovered her composure, the lead said, "We suggest they be transferred to a cancer treatment center of their parent's choice. This is urgent as the cells we found are fast acting."

Devastated, Susan left to say good bye to her two sweethearts. It was two hours before she could face the girls.

Caroline and Judith Ann were transferred to a Cancer Treatment Center, and both girls died one month later within hours of each other.

Susan was heartbroken. She could hardly wait to fly home and talk with her father. She desperately needed advice.

"I'm contemplating a transfer after the end of the year."

"Where to?"

"Georgetown University," she said. "I will finish my bachelors and work toward my masters degree in medical science."

"What are the advantages and disadvantages? The pros and cons?"

Susan started to cry. "It has nothing to do with pros and cons!" she yelled. "I just can't stay where the memories of Caroline and Judith Ann are so strong."

Her father said, very matter of fact, "You may go anywhere you choose. What is the problem?"

She sat down, looking defeated. "Tuition at Notre Dame is paid. George Washington University will cost $35,000 to $40,000 per semester."

"When will you need the money?"

"I'm not sure yet," she informed him. "I'm going to negotiate for a deal similar to the one she had at Notre Dame."

Carl studied his daughter for a moment. "I will transfer the money to your account," he finally said. "You can do whatever you like with it."

Susan was stunned. She had not anticipated her father's acceptance of her independent life. "Thank you," she said, finally able to choke out the words. "I will be forever grateful."

She departed for Notre Dame to finish the semester and to contact George Washington University officials.

Susan wondered if she was being strategic or being a coward, but her mind eased when George Washington University approved her application and offered the same financial she received from Notre Dame. They expressed delight that Susan would consider their university for her studies. When she mentioned changing her major, however, they suddenly became opposed.

"What are you considering as a major then?"

"Probably not medical science, but something associated with medicine. I just need a break. When someone mentions cancer or death due to cancer, I get so emotional. It was so sad to lose Caroline and Judith Ann. It still is."

***

Susan made plans to meet with Cassidy. When he arrived, they made arrangements for the two of them to stay at a friend's house for the weekend. Since Susan was looking forward to a relaxing visit, she moved everything from her schedule.

Cassidy was not fully prepared for how possessive Susan was. She wanted to monopolize his time, and he did not respond well. By noon on Saturday, he informed her he was leaving for Laramie.

Disappointed, Susan left a message for her friends thanking them for the accommodations. As she locked the door, she sat on the porch steps and cried.

Susan returned to her dorm at Notre Dame and began to pack in preparation for her move to Washington D.C. She took a break to walk through the neighborhood and think about Caroline and Judith Ann and reconsider her decision to leave the medical field.

And she thought of Cassidy. She reflected on her with him and asked herself if she was to blame for a man's attitude. Then she thought that, perhaps, she was related to her mother.

She ended up at the student union. Sitting at a table alone merely advertised that she was lonely, and it didn't take long before three guys asked to sit with her. Susan enjoyed her conversation, however, she began to feel as though she didn't belong. She excused herself.

At her dorm room, Susan opened her textbook and decided to work on her last examination before announcing to anyone her intent to leave the university. She read the material over and felt confident that she was ready.

The day of the examination, she was dressed to the nines and decided she was going to be aggressive and not surrender a point unless it would serve her grade. Four students were asked to present before Susan.

When it was her turn, she took her position behind the podium and greeted the class. Soon, she began to challenge each member on how to grieve when one experienced the loss of loved ones—especially patients. When the presentation was finished, most students asked questions while others could not speak through their tears. The instructor acknowledged Susan in an open and respectful manner. He assured her that her grade was outstanding.

Susan sat down and noticed she was perspiring profusely. As soon as the class was excused, she headed for the rest room where she dried herself, preparing for the next class. As she left the ladies room, she was confronted with her entire class who had been waiting to congratulate her on her success during the presentation. There were hugs around for everyone except one gentleman who asked her for a date.

Susan was stunned by the reaction of her classmates, and she told them so before returning to her room.

Suddenly, she laughed at the idea that her mother had inspired her to search for a virile man for her satisfaction, and she ended up without one candidate.

"How lucky is that?" she asked the empty room.

It was time to start packing for her trip to Georgetown. She was looking forward to the drive to D.C. She made one last look at her room, satisfied herself that she had everything in the car, locked the door and returned her room key to the University.

Susan departed the University of Notre Dame with straight As. She called Cassidy to tell him she was relocating.

Sounding distant, he said, "I'm planning to attend another rodeo in Fort Worth, Texas." He then corrected himself. "That is, when I get out of this hospital."

"The hospital!"

"Yeah. My last rodeo was a rough ride."

***

Arriving in Washington D.C., Susan called her father and informed him she had successfully negotiated a tuition-free course of study at Georgetown. She explained that it might take one semester longer than she had planned.

"I have every confidence in your abilities," her father said, "and I do not worry about anything you do."

"Thanks," Susan said. She hesitated and then asked, "Are you and Mother getting along better?"

"Your mother thinks I do not know what is going on with Alfred. I've known for years. It will probably continue until Martha tires of him," Carl said. "If you want to discuss your mother's personal habits, give me a call, because I do not want you to do the same."

Susan got up the courage to ask, "Are you having an affair?"

Without taking a pause, Carl replied, "I have five or six women that meet my needs."

She gasped. "Five or six?" She was stunned. Suddenly, she lost all respect for her father.

The revelation sent Susan to a local club which advertised in the local campus paper. She found a vacant booth which she occupied.

"What would you like to drink?" the server asked.

Still not twenty-one, Susan was glad the waitress hadn't asked for I.D. "I'll take a Jack and Coke. And yes to the idea of food."

The hostess served her drink and provided a menu. Within seconds, she was approached by two guys looking for some action.

"Can we buy you a drink?"

Susan liked her first impression and decided to extend her stay. Their conversation was friendly, and the exchange of information reflected a positive opinion of the university and the professors.

"So you are students?"

"Seniors now," one of the men said.

"How is the grading?" Susan asked.

"Depends on the professor. Are you looking for an apartment?"

Susan knew the guys were hunting girls. "Maybe," she said before excusing herself and returning to her room.

The phone rang, and Susan refused to answer it. She preferred the quiet of her apartment and no questions. She slept for a long time.

***

While meeting with the placement counselor at Georgetown University, Susan was asked to declare her major and minor. Medical science was still interesting, however she was still haunted by her memories of Caroline and Judith Ann. She sometimes dreamed of the two girls, and the dreams always ended negatively. Accordingly, she thought she should pursue another study and brought this matter to the counselor. The counselor suggested the study of Medical Science Law with a Minor in Psychology.

"We'll need to evaluate the number of hours required to finish your degree," the counselor said.

Susan thought she had experienced her first challenge, and she was excited. Entering Dizzy's Dugout, Susan met several students. They asked about her plan to transition from medical science to an emphasis on medical science law. When she gave her explanation, she saw the students' eyes glaze over as they went silent. She concluded she was in the wrong crowd and changed the subject.

After several minutes had passed, one student asked to speak with her regarding the change in major. Susan moved to another booth, and Richard introduced himself.

"I hope you don't mind. I called a friend to come join us."

Richard explained that both his friend and he were transitioning from one major to another, and he wanted to help her avoid some pitfalls.

"Thank you," Susan said. "Can I buy you lunch?"

When Richard's friend Theresa arrived, they ordered food and drinks. Susan informed her new friends precisely what she was planning and asked if they thought it wise to embark on such a field of study. During their conversation, Susan detected a significant degree of concern for the cost of their education.

"I'm in debt close to one hundred and fifty thousand," Theresa said. "And I haven't graduated yet. Richard owes two hundred and sixty even though he found a job to help with expenses."

"Are the interest rates low, at least?"

"Low for now," Theresa responded, "but it will increase significantly upon graduation."

***

Susan listened to the counselor and reviewed the details involved in the transition to a medical science lawyer curriculum. She was impressed with the courses she would need, and she asked about university funding. The counselor had done his research and confirmed full payment of expenses by Georgetown University, including a tour of several law firms required for graduation.

Arriving at Reagan International Airport, Susan took a cab to her apartment. Looking at the stack of books on the table was depressing until she opened one of them and could feel the excitement swelling inside her. She was ready, and nothing was going to stop her from becoming the best medical lawyer in the U.S.

"Nothing but myself," she said to the empty room.

It was three p.m. in D.C. on a lazy Sunday afternoon. Susan had already scanned the three books she would need for class the next day. Her ability to read text material and never forget it was a tremendous benefit. She was going after the best grade the professor could offer. She also hoped for competition in the classroom as it caused her to dedicate herself to be better. It was not in the cards for Susan to come in second to other women. She didn't even think about competing with the men. She wondered why.

Susan received a call from William, a student in one of the law classes.

"I'd like to ask you to have lunch," he said.

As soon as they met, Susan discovered she was attracted to William. He was talkative and demonstrated a great interest in Susan. They discussed their backgrounds. She wondered if William was telling the truth as she did not know such common people existed.

Following lunch, William had a class to attend and asked to get together the next day. Susan actually became excited about her first date at Georgetown. She returned to her apartment and laid on the bed to nap, but couldn't sleep for thinking of William. Susan lounged in her bed and let her mind wander. The extra glass of wine she drank did nothing to relieve her new feelings.

Three of Susan's professors assigned reading material that Susan considered a waste of her time. She passed the first tests in each class with a hundred percent on each exam.

Susan committed herself to a full effort toward academic achievement. She looked forward to new associations, new issues, new friends and new subjects. In each classroom, she chose to sit toward the middle of the rows—hoping to get lost among the students. For some reason, she felt the urge to be alone in a crowd, to hide in the weeds and observe the class before she committed herself to a particular role. She could not explain her feelings, but she had to acknowledge them. Often, Cassidy came to mind, demanding her attention. Life on the rodeo circuit frightened her, especially since his most recent accident.

***

Professor Freeman—a practicing attorney and enthusiastic supporter of the right to die—entered the classroom and informed the class they could expect a research assignment toward midterm. The students' research should explore theories as to why people should or should not be allowed a choice as to their death. Susan thought this was different than any course she had taken, and she wondered if she was in the right course. She continued listening and began to understand that the professor was providing an advanced outline of the course he was going to teach. The second issue was medical ethics in our time, followed by litigation and the courts.

Susan left the class and headed home for a drink and a quiet place to study. She opened three of her books and began to read. Absorbed in the subject matter, she continued to read until past midnight. Relaxing on her bed, Susan began to think about ways she could become advanced in law of various issues.

She awakened at the sound of her cell phone. "Hello?"

"Hi. It's Jeffrey. I'm in your pre-law class."

"Jeffrey. Yes, hi."

They began to discuss the upcoming assignments when Susan changed the subject.

"I'm curious. Why are you taking pre-law?"

"I've completed an undergraduate degree," he said. "A Juris Doctor diploma. I'm now studying for the state's bar examination."

"Really?" Susan was quiet a moment. "I'm beginning to wonder if I'm pursuing the wrong program."

"Do you have your JD?"

"No, my studies were concentrated in the medical field."

"And now you are considering law?"

"Not initially," she said. "But I'm intrigued by the subject of *right to die*. I'm wondering if the question should be considered by more distinguished members of the cloth. Or at least a psychiatrist or psychologist. Even a personal physician familiar with the circumstances would have more insight than a lawyer."

"But the lawyers are only responsible for setting up the legality. Life and death is not really their decision to make," Jeffrey said, hoping to assuage her concerns.

"Perhaps," she admitted. "But it's all so final and distasteful."

Susan took her concerns to her school counselor who informed her that she should establish a structured course of study to obtain her objective. She called her father and had a long and beneficial discussion regarding her goal—whatever that happened to be.

"I'm sorry, Dad. I'm still not sure what my goal is. I believe one should believe so strongly in God's power that we should let God take care of it, regardless."

"It is time for you to decide that issue," he said.

Susan began to research the subject of child medicine and determined she should embark on a broadly structured course which would assist her in legal skills, contracts, and torts. This would give her a range of knowledge in civil liability, negligence, strict liability and intentional wrongdoing. The final goal was a Master of Laws specialized degree.

She called Jeffrey to let him know her decision and to ask him to dinner so they could go over her research as she wanted his opinion.

When they met at a nice restaurant, Jeffery commented, "I'm so happy you are buying. I'm hungry and broke!"

They discussed Susan's goal, and Jeffery was overwhelmed. He expressed doubt that anyone could complete all that study in ten years.

"I will do it in five," Susan boasted.

Susan focused on her goal, coordinated it with her counselor, and discussed in detail how she intended to complete the college work she had laid out for herself. Thinking of the next semester, she realized how difficult a schedule she had developed. She knew she was self-disciplined, oriented toward achievement of the difficult and, yes, she had an eccentric personality. Her self-analysis pleased her. The depth to which she believed in herself, bordered on conviction. She genuinely wanted to excel in the treatment of the young and innocent.

Early the next morning, she walked to class feeling good about herself. She ran into Jeffrey, and they chatted. As they walked into the classroom, she thought about the fact that he had not once suggested they be affectionate, and she asked herself why. Just for the fun of it, she made plans to proposition him and see how he reacted.

Legal Skills was another waste of her time. The professor made assignments and then left. Susan used the time to study, but the professor's attitude about class time irritated her. The more she thought about it, the more it affected her thinking and her attitude. Realizing she was becoming angry only worsened her situation. Wanting to ease her stress, she walked to the student union and sat with some friends, remaining quiet while she drank a soda.

To her surprise, Jeffrey walked in, and immediately her attitude improved.

"Did you hear about the strike?" he asked.

"No. What strike?"

"Several of the professors decided on a three-day strike. Pay and such."

Frustrated, Susan left the student union. She did not handle down-time well, so she decided to immerse herself in the subjects she had selected. She began to read every document available on legal skills, and contracts tort law. After three days of concentrated reading—and an empty refrigerator—she made a trip to the local grocery store to purchase sufficient food for a month. Getting back to the books had become exhilarating and rewarding.

She also thought of Cassidy.

"Hey," she said when he answered the phone. "How about a three-day hiatus to immerse ourselves in each other and throw caution to the wind? Especially a strong wind."

***

When the strike had ended, Susan arrived early for her classes and found several of her classmates wondering in and out of the hallway. She found her seat and opened her text book to review the chapter. Another student approached and asked if he could sit beside her during class.

"Sure," she told him. "I'm Susan. And you are…?"

"Adam. I've been meaning to ask you for a while if you would like to go to dinner."

"I'd love to," she said, smiling at him. "One thing, though. I'm needing to stop at the library after class."

"Sure. I could look up a few things myself."

"What are you studying?"

"I am doing research on a great subject—sex and the college student."

Susan looked startled. "The only time I think of sex is when I cannot concentrate."

When he noticed her discomfort, Adam asked what her area of study was.

"I have three specialties I'm concentrating on."

His eyes widened. "Are you suicidal?"

They both laughed.

Susan attended her psychology class and asked the professor if she could test out for credit. He scheduled the examination for the following week and, on Thursday, she passed with flying colors. This gave her the courage to ask about testing out on every subject the university approved. She completed seven courses through this process, three in psychology and four in contract law.

Susan scheduled a meeting with her counselor and prepared to receive a lecture as to the expedited completion of several courses. Upon arrival, the counselor was quiet for several minutes.

"I do not know what to say to you," she finally said. "I think I should say 'do this your way' and ask you to tell me so I can get it approved. Do you think that will work?"

Susan said yes and left the office, but as she began to think more about it, she realized that she should seek the counselor's wisdom or that could result in a terrible mistake. She stopped in the middle of the walkway, turned around and returned to the counselor's office

"I'm sorry," she said, walking back into the room.

The counselor offered her a cup of coffee and asked her to take a seat.

"I'm sure you are aware of how unusual your skills and abilities are."

Susan nodded. "I've always been a bit of an eccentric. But I'm trying my best to succeed at everything I do."

"Maybe you moderate your efforts a bit."

"I'm trying," Susan replied.

"Do you have any hobbies?"

Susan brightened. "I like to read, and sometimes I like to imagine solving child cancer issues."

"I mean something besides textbooks." She gave Susan a slight smile.

"It's Caroline and Judith Ann."

"Who?"

Susan explained about the two young girls and their health issues. Before she finished, she was crying.

"We must focus our efforts toward a solution, and I intend to do just that."

"So, what motivated you to take courses in medical law practice?"

"The things I saw the doctors do that were unnecessary."

The counselor eyes the student sympathetically. "I will confer with my superiors to see how many classes you can test out of. Are you going to study case law?"

Susan replied, "Yes. I will enroll in one course in each discipline and advance my reading of the different case laws until I get the feeling of each. I think the university would look at my effort more favorably than if I had asked before completing each course."

"I just worry that you're rushing everything too much. There is such a thing as burnout."

Susan replied, "Counselor, to me everything is excessively slow. I want to go fast and do it all. I simply cannot wait for the cows to come home. I must go get them today and bring them home, do you understand?"

"You are very complex, and I admit I do not understand you. However, I will confer with my colleagues, and will get back to you."

Walking back to the dorm, Susan began to think of ways to deal with her frustration. She hurried to her room, poured a Jack Daniels and drank it straight. Three hours passed before she moved. When she tried to raise her head, she realized she had consumed too much alcohol and returned to sleep.

***

Months later, Susan had tested through several courses in medical science, legal skills, tort law and a preparatory course to prepare for the state bar examination. She conferred with her counselor and was approved to complete all requirements for the bachelor of science degree, and she tested out for her masters in psychology.

"Is it true that you are working part time for a group of lawyers specializing in childhood diseases?" her counselor asked.

"Yes," Susan replied. "Though, most of my time is spent observing experienced lawyers in their effort to attend specific trials involving lawsuits related to childhood medical practices."

"Remind me how old you are."

"I'll be twenty this year," Susan said.

"And how long have you been attending Georgetown?"

"Fifteen months."

The counselor leaned on her desk and studied the young woman. "And just how long has it been since you took time for herself?"

Susan replied, "I think about seven or eight months."

After she left the meeting, she called her father. When he answered, she merely said, "Beach house in one week."

Her father replied, "You are on. No conflicts, no restrictions, just plain fun." Then he added, "You must be smiling. I can tell."

"I may have a surprise to tell you, but we shall see."

The testing was difficult, and Susan wondered if she had made a good decision. She thought she could have used a couple months more with the attorneys to assist her confidence, but that was too late. So she concentrated on the issues at hand and completed the seven tests in one week.

When she received her grades, she returned to the counselor to share the information.

"Susan, we have never had a student who possessed the qualities you demonstrate. Your accomplishments have been remarkable, and you should be recognized for them. But again, I would be remiss if I did not caution you on the distinct possibility of burn out. Personally, I cannot understand how you can withstand the stress. I understand what you want to accomplish, however I believe you risk repercussions to your health and well-being."

"To ease your mind," Susan said, "I'm going to a beach house next week for some relaxation."

When she walked outside, she raised a clenched fist and yelled at the top of her voice, "All effort straight ahead, and no one can stop us!"

***

Arriving at the beach house, Susan was surprised to learn her father had arranged for a choice of drinks and delicious food. She was determined to have her fun, but she also wanted to relax with walks on the beach to feel the sand between her toes. She quickly put on her beach shoes and a pair of shorts and took a walk along the water's edge. Periodically, Susan stopped and viewed the lake water, watching the waves and dreaming. She considered her last conversation with the counselor when they determined that Harvard Law should be her next step. Susan stared at the water and began to dream when her father walked up beside her.

"Hi," he said. "What's on your mind."

"Nothing," she said. "What's going on with you?"

They talked as if they had not seen each other in years. Susan wanted to listen more than talk and to relax. Within minutes of returning to the house, Susan was asleep on the sofa.

Carl made good use of the bedroom, opened the window and went to sleep.

When they awoke the next morning, Susan told her father that she'd invited her counselor Daren for an evening at the lake. "The two of you can hash out my future," she teased.

When Daren arrived, Carl extended a warm welcome. They all enjoyed a lovely dinner and then took a bottle of whiskey with them to the lake shore and built a bonfire.

During a long walk on the beach after sunset, Susan noticed that her father and Daren seemed to have a connection. The realization brought back conflicting feelings about her parents and their inability to satisfy each other. She put her thoughts aside as they all retired for the night.

Late the next morning, Daren joined others on the deck for coffee and Danish.

"What a lovely retreat," she told Susan. "I am more relaxed than I've been in a long time." Daren glanced at Carl, and they seemed to share a secret smile.

Susan was still thinking of her decision to attend Harvard law and Medicine schools. The actual court cases she had been monitoring caused her concern. Her confidence level was not as great as it had been studying most other cases, and that was bothering her. She went for a walk on the water's edge and relaxes to the rhythm of the waves flapping against the beach. She walked into the water and felt the soothing waves touching her feet. As she stepped farther in, the lake water caressed her body, reminding her of time spent with Cassidy.

Her father's voice jolted her out of her reverie. "I hope this trip has done you some good," he said, escorting her back to the beach house.

"A lot of good," she said, her voice sounding less than sincere. "I'm leaving today."

"But you just got here! I thought you wanted to stay a week." When she did not respond, he asked, "Is something troubling you?" He followed Susan into the bedroom she has occupied.

"I have a lot to think about and want to get on with it," she said as she started to pack.

Carl pushed a little harder. "Is this about money?"

"No. I still haven't used the forty you gave me."

He watched his daughter avoid eye contact. "You're uncomfortable with Daren and I, aren't you?"

Susan shook her head no even though she felt that was part of her concern. "I really just need to get back," she said.

***

Susan arrived for her flight to O'Hare and noticed very few seats were occupied. She spread out to occupy two seats and went to sleep. Soon, the stewardess woke her to say they had arrived.

Returning to school, Susan entered her ethics law class and chose her usual center seat. She tried to visualize herself in court as if she was trying an actual case. The professor broke her concentration by announcing the first examination. She was well prepared and did well on the test. Following class, she asked the professor her usual set of questions regarding testing out of the course. He agreed.

Susan was anxious to get through her law courses quickly, but she decided against testing out of her medical courses. She didn't want to miss important discussions and perhaps miss critical distinctions regarding medical findings that could literally mean life and death.

When Daren returned to her office, Susan talked with her about doubling up on courses in medicine. After looking them over for a few minutes, Susan interrupted.

"I don't know why you need to review them. You know they are perfect scores."

"You're right," Daren said, putting papers aside. "You certainly have no deficiency regarding your educational pursuits. You are a driven young woman."

"In more ways than one," Susan said. "But you would know what I'm talking about."

The counselor studied Susan's demeanor for a moment. "You know, I admire you a great deal. But I sense that something has changed in our relationship. Does the time I spent with your father upset you?"

"Why should it? I'm a sexual being myself."

"It wasn't very professional even though there is no policy against it. But I don't want this to interfere with my ability to counsel you."

"I bowed out of my parents' love lives a long time ago."

"Still, if this has in any way compromised your trust in me, tell me so now."

Susan shook her head. "You supported everything I've wanted to do here. My biggest concern now is that the counselor at Harvard Medical does not."

Daren frowned. "Well, I've certainly made it clear to them that you are capable. You are twenty-two years of age, have earned two masters' degrees, passed the bar exam and have tested out on thirty-six hours credit in medical school leading to licensure as a physician specializing in pediatric illnesses." She took a deep breath. "I don't know what else they would need to convince them."

"My goal," Susan said, "is to qualify for that licensure within two years. But if Harvard Medical School does not support my goals, I will enroll at Stanford Medical in the fall."

***

Susan flew to San Francisco, California and rented a car for her excursion, site seeing trip to Palo Alto and the Stanford Medical School. She was not in a hurry and wanted to enjoy her time. She called her father and asked him if he knew where she was.

"Honestly, I stopped following you a long time ago. You're a mature adult and worthy of your own ventures."

Susan had scheduled an appointment with the Stanford University Medical School and, upon arrival, she sought determination if it was possible for her to complete certification for accepting and performing pediatric physician duties. She had prepared by first determining the requirements and then comparing her own transcripts against them. However, she wanted to get a Stanford University official to tell her what she needed to do to accomplish her objective.

Upon arrival for her appointment, the counselor introduced himself as Dr. Joel Smith, dean of students. Dr. Smith asked Susan to tell him her objective and she proceeded. First, she presented a copy of her transcript and briefly stated her background, including her stay at Notre Dame, Georgetown and Harvard School of Law and Medicine.

Eyes wide, Dr. Smith asked, "How did you accomplished so much in such a short period of time?"

Susan explained, "I'm a fast reader, and I retained almost everything. It was easy for me to test out of several courses so I could move on quickly."

"This is admirable," Dr. Smith said, "but I would caution against a tendency to gloss over very important aspects of each course."

"Aren't the examinations designed to reflect the students' knowledge? Would the material covered accurately reflect the competency of a student taking the examination?"

Dr. Smith furrowed his brow. "There is more to be gleaned from a course that what comes from the textbooks. But I'm willing to administer entrance examinations on any course you want to take. After I make a more thorough review of your transcripts, I'll assist in submitting your application to attend Stanford. Will that be satisfactory?"

Susan nodded. "Dr. Smith, I am confident I can qualify for entrance to Stanford Medical School. More so, equal treatment is all I request."

She thanked Dr. Smith, offered him her personal card with contact information, located the student union and walked there for lunch. Thinking of the conversation she had with Dr. Smith, she wondered how he took her mannerisms and her insistence that she receive equal treatment by the board. Very shortly, she received a phone call asking if she was available for a briefing in the next few days on specific aspects of their program.

Candice informed her that the Board of Professors had agreed to an interview with her at 9:00 a.m. the following day. They had already conferred with the main counselor for medical school applicants, Joyce Lambert, who sounded optimistic about Susan's transcripts.

When Susan arrived the next morning, she and Candice hit it off immediately and talked about the fact that Candice had grown up in cold northern Michigan—something they had in common.

"How old are you?" Candice asked.

"I will be twenty-two next month."

"Wow. So young to be working on your doctorate. Do you ever get homesick?"

"Yes, I miss my father. I'm not very close to my mother. We do not get along well."

Candice said, "I miss both my parents and want to see them more often than it is possible."

Susan asked, "Do you fly home much?"

"I cannot afford it as much as I'd like."

"I understand, but I believe in miracles, so do not give up on hope."

Susan had prepared for a lecture from the Board of Professors, but instead, they asked her questions regarding her educational pursuits and specifically how she was able to attend the University of Notre Dame, Georgetown, and the University of Michigan and Michigan Medical School within a two-year time frame with a four-point GPA.

Susan simply responded, "It was hard work, dedication and commitment to achieve my goal of which The Stanford University School of Medicine plays an integral part. You must understand, I committed to two young ladies who died of childhood cancer. You see, I loved these two girls—Caroline and Judith Ann. We ate together, played together, shed tears together> They loved me and I loved them. They died from a disease we should be able to cure if we care enough to put forth the effort. I will dedicate my life's pursuit to improving medical treatment for young people, and the program I am now in is part of that effort." With tears in her eyes, she asked if she might take a break.

"Certainly," Dr. Lambert said.

When she returned, the board asked her questions about her methodology as her achievement was more than extraordinary. When they had finished, Dr. Lambert faced the group and said, "I recommend we participate in Susan's effort by paying her a monthly stipend of ten thousand dollars to help with her expenses."

The vote was unanimous. Susan thanked each of them and departed to contact her father. Walking to her car, she could hardly contain her enthusiasm as she knew she had completed the last hurdle of her educational pursuit with the exception of passing the California Bar exam.

When Carl answered the phone, however, Susan suspected something was wrong. After hanging up, she called her mother hoping to find out more.

"I'm sorry, honey. I should have called you sooner. Your father has had a mild stroke."

"I will catch the first flight out of San Francisco!"

"Sweetheart, it's a mild stroke. No need to worry."

"No need?" Susan was angry now. "He's my father!"

When Susan arrived in Michigan, she hurried home only to discover that Carl had had a second stroke and was hospitalized. She went directly to him and had to be consoled when she saw his face twisted almost beyond recognition.

She sought the doctor on duty and asked him to give her details about the medical attention her father required.

"We're still running diagnostic tests. It will be some time before we know the extent of the damage.

Susan returned to her father's side and held his hand. He seemed to sense her presence and smiled.

"Dad," she said, coming closer. "I'm praying for you. I hope you are seeking forgiveness for your sins."

Her father closed his eyes, but almost instantly they opened wide again, staring. Susan put his hand on his chest and walked out of the room. She stood in silence. Stunned. She understood her father had died.

***

Susan was finding it difficult to concentrate. Late in the day, when she had returned to Palo Alto, she walked leisurely across a beautiful section of the university grounds and periodically stopped to thank God for the goodness and mercy He had provided her and her family. She acknowledged her weaknesses and asked for strength and courage to complete her commitment to Caroline and Judith Ann. She rationalized that her father had lived a great life of more than seventy years, and God did him a favor by taking him home.

With tears in her eyes, she stopped and watched two doves walking along the bank of a small lake. She knew that doves mated for life, and it stirred something in her. She called her mother.

"How are you getting along?"

"I'm fine, Susan," her mother said coldly.

"What are you planning to do?"

Without a moment's hesitation, she responded, "I will find another virile man who is much younger and is striving to prove his stamina."

Susan was speechless.

Her mother continued by stating, "You don't need to concern yourself with my future."

Susan returned to her room and sat on the bed. It was difficult reflecting on the events of the last few days, but even more difficult trying to reconcile her relationship with her mother.

When the semester started and Susan entered her first classroom, she kept to her habit of choosing a seat in the center of the classroom.

The professor arrived and stated, "This is the advanced class for genics, and I am wondering if everyone belongs in this class."

Three students immediately stood and left. When things settled again, the professor made reading assignments for the entire semester, including research material which could be found at the library. He stated it would be wise for everyone to read the entire textbook list for the course plus the research referred to on page nine of the course outline.

"I will not hold class on any Friday throughout the entire semester. I expect you to use this time wisely to research and study the material."

Susan glanced at the first chapter. This would be the first step in understanding the human DNA and could possibly lead to diagnosing the issues faced by Caroline and Julia Ann.

Returning to her room, Susan became despondent thinking about the death of her father. This was the third person she had been close to who had died. She also realized that she no one to lean on. Then she thought of Cassidy. She wished the two of them could find a way to build on something besides sex.

Susan knew very little about the grieving process. She fully believed that she move on from the loss of her father. Anger took over. She poured her anger into the research assignment she had been given, and ignored her feelings.

She finished the reading assignment before noon. She had already studied the textbook and did not find it difficult. She was now perplexed at her perception of the course so, at the conclusion of the next class in genics, she asked the professor if it was permissible to test out.

"If you think you can," he responded. "No second chances."

After administering the test, he requested they meet to discuss the next step.

"I've never graded a paper before where I could not fine one mistake. If I hadn't been watching you, I would have assumed you cheated."

Susan stiffened. "I've never cheated."

"No. I don't suppose you have. As far as I'm concerned, you can test out of any course that I'm responsible for."

When she relaxed her shoulders, he added, "I'd like to invite you to attend dinner with me and two of my colleagues. They are faculty you should get to know."

"Thank you, Professor Goodyear."

"Do you know the Old Student Groan? It's a famous eatery that has been in business here for many years."

"I'll find it," she said.

The dinner was great, and Susan enjoyed the conversation with the three professors. She excused herself early to prepare for class the next day.

Pediatric Oncology, she believed, could have prevented the deaths of Caroline and Julia Ann, though in her early studies, Susan had guarded herself against drawing conclusions prematurely. This particular class would study treatment options such as immunotherapy, chemotherapy, and stem cell transplant. The treatment used on a patient would depend on the diagnosis and pediatric radiation. Susan was excited about becoming involved in courses dealing with the illness that took the lives of her two sweethearts.

The Pediatric Oncology professor introduced himself as Jack Lawless. At the end of class, he asked if he could have an extensive conversation with Susan about her achievements. She shared her brief stays at her previous schools and now Stanford.

"Can I ask why you jump from one organization to another? Is it truly for your studies, or are you running from something or someone?"

Susan lost her smile. "There is none of that," she insisted. "I have a desire to excel, and I don't take no for an answer."

"Exactly how old are you?" Jack asked.

"How old do you think I am?"

Jack recounted her educational history and finally said, "I would venture a guess of thirty-three."

"How embarrassing! Do you think I look like I am thirty-three?"

"You look nineteen, but your achievements tell a different story."

"Professor, I will be twenty-two this month."

During their talk, Susan discovered he had a brother who had died from a form of cancer which had, to date, remained unknown. David had died of cancer, diabetes and whiskey consumption.

"I'm so sorry," she said. "Two years ago, I accepted responsibility for two lovely young ladies who were each ten years old and suffering from a form of cancer. They died while under my care. I wanted so desperately to help them, which is why I am motivated to do something about it."

"Looks like we have that in common," Jack said.

"I have chosen genics to broaden my studies and hopefully assist in solving some of the critical issues surrounding the various forms of cancer."

"Perhaps we could form a team and work together," Jack suggested.

"You as Professor of Oncology and me as a future Professor in Pediatric Genetics. Is that an idea, or is it?"

Jack hugged Susan and then backed away. "I'm sorry. That was totally inappropriate considering you are one of my students."

After she left Jack, Susan realized how lonely she was, but she wanted to talk to someone not involved in educational pursuits. She called, and Cassidy answered immediately.

"How are you?" he asked.

"Lonesome."

"Me, too," he said. "I'm in Laramie, Wyoming."

"Another rodeo?"

"Nah. I was homesick, and I wanted to see my mother and grandfather. It's seventeen below zero and the wind is howling. I've taken a job on a ranch until spring when the rodeo circuit starts up again."

Susan filled him in on her move and the classwork coming up.

"I miss you," he said when she finished. "Your call makes me want to meet up."

"Maybe soon," she said before ending the call.

***

Susan left the classroom and walked to the Student Union hoping to establish a casual relationship with some of the other students. She had began to think of herself as an outcast. Even thoughts of Cassidy didn't fill her with comfort. It was time to push a little harder for a connection with other students.

Dr, Lambert found her sitting alone and asked how she felt about Stanford and her progress to date.

"Classes are going very well," Susan told her. "I have not made any friends yet, but that will change with time."

"There is a student mixer coming up. Perhaps that would be a place to make some new acquaintances. Faculty, food, and drink. What could be better?"

Susan arrived late to the event, but on time to participate in the get-acquainted festivities. Jack was there lingering near the refreshment bar. When the music began, he asked her to the dance floor.

Later in the evening, a student asked Susan to dance. She ended her evening on a light note and promise to have dinner with Harry soon.

As Susan entered her apartment, she reflected on the evening and knew immediately that there was something special about Harry. She loved his mannerisms, and she had felt a tingle every time he touched her. Opening the textbooks, she had planned to study, but thoughts of Harry continued to distract her. Setting the book aside, Susan let herself think of a life she had ignored for several months and wondered if she had lost interest in loving someone.

Memories of her late father sprang up, and the tears began to flow. Following a good cry, she washed her face and sat thinking of her mother and the conflict that existed between them.

Refusing to dwell on it, she decided to give Harry a call and was thrilled when he answered.

"I hope it's not too late to call," she said.

"Not at all. I'm glad you did."

"I just wanted to say that I hadn't had that much fun in a long time."

They enjoyed a long conversation, agreeing to meet the next day for lunch.

Susan remembered his touch. "I'm not sure I can wait until tomorrow."

"I could come over tonight, if you want. But I do have to study for a test tomorrow at 8:00 a.m."

Susan kept quiet about testing out of so many courses. What came easy to her was not so easy for others, and she didn't want him to feel awkward. "I'll see you tomorrow for lunch, then," she said before hanging up.

***

Susan met with Dr. Lambert to discuss her progress.

"I've been considering the fact that genics is an excessively narrow field, considering your background. I'd like you to attend an annual event sponsored by the university. The Friday luncheon honors personnel from the local hospital who had been recognized for outstanding achievement in their assigned specialty in the field of pediatric medicine."

"The luncheon sounds lovely," Susan replied, "I will give your suggestions serious consideration, but I'm not ready to change my focus. If you did have a recommendation, what would that be?"

"Pediatric medicine," Dr. Lambert told her. "Susan, you are well positioned academically to pursue that study, and Stanford will be awarding five lucky students large grants to assume in-depth studies of childhood diseases."

Susan left the office as her mind whirled with thoughts about changing her pursuit and all that was involved in that decision. She began to think of the different specialties—podiatry, neonatal, oncology, gynecology, pediatric surgery and cardiology. Her mind was so consumed with her thoughts that she passed Harry on the sidewalk without speaking.

"Where are you going in such a hurry?" he asked.

"Oh, Harry. Sorry I didn't see you."

"Want to meet for lunch again on Friday?"

"I can't. I have a previous engagement." She made her escape and retreated to her room.

Friday's luncheon was a formal affair. Susan sat with Dr. Lambert who introduced her around to the medical professionals at their table. After the meal, Susan expected to see five of her classmates introduced during the awards presentation. She was shocked when her own name was called as one of the grant recipients.

When she returned to her seat, Dr. Lambert hugged her. "I didn't want to spoil the surprise, but I had nominated you for the grant. I was so hoping you wouldn't turn down the invitation to the luncheon."

"Thank you so much," Susan kept saying as she stared at the plaque they had given her. "Remind me again, how much is the grant?"

"One million. That should fund a great deal of research."

Susan floated through the rest of the afternoon and evening. Realizing late that she hadn't had dinner, she called Harry and asked him over to her place for pizza.

"I can't believe it," he said when she him told about the grant. "That's fantastic!"

"It is," she agreed, "but it means I will have to change my class schedule for the coming semester. Dr. Lambert says I'm making the right decision. But it feels strange."

"Are you worried it will add years to your coursework?"

For the first time, Susan told Harry about her academic career and how young she was. When she finished, he sat silent contemplating how she could have achieved all that she had.

"I have the full support of the university in this," she assured him.

He studied her face. "Why do I get the feeling you're not sure about all this?"

She nodded. "You are right. I'm not sure. This award makes things so much more complex. Up to now, the decisions have been all mine. The grant complicates things. The committee will have its own set of expectations, and they might want to influence what direction I take. What if I lose sight of what brought me to medicine in the first place?"

"There's only one way to find out," he said. "Talk to Dr. Lambert on Monday."

***

In the two years since Susan had accepted her grant for research, she became more involved in Stanford Medical's program sponsoring young children suffering from various forms of cancer. She elected to enter into a research program wherein young students who had been selected for special trial programs were being treated with experimental drugs and observed to measure progress in cancer growth. Working the program delayed the achievement of her doctorate, but the experience held great potential in her field.

Susan had also inherited five million from her father's estate. The reading of the will had been the last time she had seen her mother or her siblings. On returning from Michigan, Susan had wondered about her young life and the fact that she had no one important meeting her at the airport. She had briefly considered entering into a relationship with Harry, but he too would have been too much of a distraction from her purpose.

As it was, Susan's entire waking hours were focused on her research. She arrived at her apartment late most nights—tired and somewhat depressed that the medical studies were not producing results faster.

One thing she could control was her education. She decided to talk with Dr. Lambert about speeding up her coursework for her doctorate in pediatric medicine and to explore the requirements for residency.

"You don't slow down, do you?" Dr. Lambert quipped, and then she frowned. "I'm seriously worried that you are headed for a crash of your own making. Your mind and body can only take so much."

Susan dropped her eyes to the floor. "I don't know how to pull back. It's not my nature."

Joyce paused and then asked, "Do you recall the instructions you get about oxygen masks during an emergency aboard an airplane?"

Susan nodded.

"And what instructions do they give the parents?"

Susan was annoyed by the question, but she answered, "Put on your mask and then help your child."

"My dear, you are the parent. The best way to help the children is to make sure you have the oxygen you need first."

It took a moment for Dr. Lambert's message to sink in, but then Susan smiled. "Joyce, you are the best person I have ever known."

"Just promise me you will take care of yourself so that you can then take care of others."

Susan excused herself and left the office. As she walked to her car, she reflected on Joyce's words. Harry came to mind. The two had not spent time together since her grant came through, but she saw him on campus from time to time. Taking a chance that he had not found someone else, she gave him a call.

"I have something to show you if you have some free time," she told him.

"For you," he said, "I always have free time."

"Meet me at the union."

When Harry arrived, Susan stepped out of her new Cadillac. He walked the length of the car, examining it from one end to the other.

"Let's take it for a spin," she said.

Susan turned the car on and then reached over and ran her fingers through Harry's hair.

"This is not what I was expecting," he said.

She turned on the music and then leaned in for a passionate kiss. As Harry began to respond, the car quit running.

"Shit!" Susan cried out. "I forgot to get gas."

They were silent for a moment, and then they both started laughing. Harry made a trip to the nearest convenience store for a gas can and some fuel.

Susan drove them to the ocean where they spent some time on the beach.

"I have to find a way to slow down," she admitted. "Doctor's orders."

"We could take a weekend trip down the coast," Harry suggested.

"That won't do. I'm thinking of taking a semester off and traveling to places I've only dreamed of up till now." She turned to him. "You should come. I don't want to travel alone."

Harry was intrigues by the idea. "I'd love to, but I don't have the money. And I'm not sure what that would do to my scholarships."

"Money is no object. I know someone."

***

As much as Susan and Harry wanted to enjoy each other on their trip, Susan could not get her research out of her mind. She became overly anxious to return to the university to resume her studies. At one point, she opened up about Caroline and Julia Ann, but it hard for her to control her emotions.

"I'm sorry for my weakness," she said. "I was hoping this trip would help me heal."

"I wouldn't call it weakness, but I do worry that you are testing out on too many subjects. There is value in the debates that occur in the classroom."

"Are you questioning my abilities? I'm a straight A student!"

"I'm not questioning your knowledge," he assured her. "It's just that you are missing out on the personal component of medicine. And maybe life." He looked at her longingly. "I know you asked me along as an escort of sorts, but I'm wondering if you have ever been intimate with a man."

"Yes. Years ago. But he was a distraction from my goals."

Looking hurt, Harry asked, "Am I a distraction?"

She left the question unanswered for the rest of their trip.

Returning to the classroom and the demands of her education, Susan regained her enthusiasm for what she had missed. She had chosen her thesis subject and just needed approval. Luckily, she had only one more class to take before she could then defend her doctorate.

Dr. Lambert called Susan with an offer to participate in a two-year effort to conduct research at the university in treating childhood cancer patients.

"This would be a salaried position and require a commitment of the full two years. You'd be treating living children who have been diagnosed with terminal cancer."

Susan hesitated. "I'm interested, but I want to discuss several matters with you before I say yes."

Dr. Lambert answered her questions. "I've specifically requested from the National Institute of Health that the university be awarded this opportunity specifically because you are ready to play a major role."

"Then I have to say yes."

While Susan was watching TV later that evening, Cassidy called.

"You'll never believe this, but I'm in San Francisco! Can I take you to dinner?"

Susan suggested a reputable restaurant recommended by a couple of friends. They enjoyed their evening, and Susan promised she had something important to discuss with him at some point in the future.

"You certainly know how to keep my interest at top level."

***

Dr. Lambert arranged for Susan to attend a National Institute of Health Conference in Chicago. The focus was "Treating Childhood Cancer." The four-day conference was fast-paced with presenters schooled in a variety of subjects.

Upon her return from Chicago, Susan tested out of her final course.

Early the next morning, Susan awakened with a large appetite. She went to a local restaurant and ordered a large breakfast. While eating, she noticed a lawyer she had met on the plane back from Chicago. Gerald sat in another section of the restaurant, and she watched him for a while to determine if he was with someone. Susan decided he was alone and walked over to his table.

"Are you alone?"

"Yes. Would you like to join me?"

Their conversation turned to Gerald's line of work. He was considering a potential position with a large manufacturer of cancer treatment drugs, and he asked Susan for her opinion.

"My training is focused on the treatment of children, but I'm skeptical of drug manufacturers as their business models were aimed toward the almighty dollar versus the health of the child." She took a sip of her coffee and then asked, "When are you expecting to make a decision regarding the job?"

He frowned and said, "It is out of Chicago, and I am not looking favorably on the cold, nasty winters they have each year. I much prefer this shirt sleeve weather we experience here every day."

"I agree." She tilted her head and then asked, "Would you like to take a walk through the park?"

Gerald indicated he would as long as they could be back within a couple of hours as he had an appointment with his doctor to have a physical.

"Routine, or is there something wrong? If I'm not being too personal."

"I wish it was only routine," he replied.

During their walk through the park, Susan noticed how distant Gerald was and decided he was not interested in her. Returning to her car, she told herself that she had been desperate to resolve her loneliness which made her blush.

Returning to her apartment, she called Dr. Lambert and invited her to dinner.

Joyce settled in and then told Susan something that brightened her mood. "I wanted to tell you that the research program offered by Stanford Medical is similar in many ways to a doctoral residency. Successful completion would also satisfy that requirement."

Susan smiled. "So if the research program comes to Stanford, I would be completing my educational requirement in six years at the age of twenty-four with a Doctorate in Pediatric Medicine. I owe much of this progress to you, Joyce."

"The program would not start for another three months. What will you do with your time?"

"Start reviewing the material, of course. You know me. And I'll have completed my thesis, given my dissertation, and graduated with honors by then."

***

Susan decided to relocate to a nicer apartment if the university was selected for the research program. She contacted a Mr. Yardley with a real estate firm to see what was available for either rent or purchase. She found three excellent choices but realized she could not make a decision until the Board of Governors made a decision in her favor.

Susan was, in fact, awarded her doctorate. She contemplated taking a vacation but still hesitated traveling alone. While discussing her situation with her Realtor, Mr. Yardley offered to let her use his beachfront condo free for a week.

Arriving at the beach house, she decided to take a stroll without shoes. Dressed in shorts and a blouse, she walked and sat overlooking the waves as they slapped at her feet. She enjoyed the rhythm of the ocean as she watched people stroll leisurely by, but it was not enough to overcome her feelings of loneliness. She reached down and scribbled a message in the sand only to have a wave wash it away.

Watching it disappear, she wondered if there was a message that she was missing. A brief rain shower served to remind her that Mother Nature was still in command.

She returned to her beach house to find a gentleman knocking on her front door. Susan asked if she could assist the gentleman.

"Is Mr. Yardley here?"

"Not right now," Susan said. "Can I give him a message?"

"I'm Arthur Gateway from Stanford University Medical School, and I am looking for Mr. Yardley."

Susan invited him in and offered him a drink. "I just graduated with my doctorate from Stanford. What do you do at the University?"

They had a long conversation, after which Mr. Gateway offered to buy her dinner.

"I'd be happy to accompany you," she said. "I know a lovely place nearby."

Arthur knew his way around the area and directed the to a nice bistro. As the waiter delivered menus, Arthur proceeded to order drinks for both himself and Susan. After taking one sip, she realized she was in for a relaxing evening.

A few moments later, Arthur asked if she liked beef or fish.

"Tonight I prefer beef."

Again, Arthur took the lead and ordered fillets for both of them.

"So, what do you need with Mr. Yardley?" she finally asked.

"I'd like to divest my real estate holdings. I've done this work since I was nineteen, and I'm tired. I want to travel through Europe and Asia."

Also, I own each building and in one year the depreciation schedule will expire causing grief for the owner unless it is sold to a new owner who can start with new depreciation schedules. Susan asked how much he was asking for each building and he replied one million if we make a deal without commissions. Susan asked what his bottom dollar was and he replied $800,000.00 each but I do not want Mr. Yardley to know that. Susan asked if Arthur had a manager taking care of the buildings to which Arthur said yes but he wants a pay raise and I do not want to increase his salary.

Susan completed her dinner and offered to dance with Arthur. The evening passed quickly.

"Do you have a place to stay for the night?" Susan asked.

When he said no, she offered him the spare room in the Mr. Yardley's house. They accompanied each other to the beach-front unit and spent an enjoyable time well into the early morning.

For breakfast, Susan had prepared bacon, eggs, toast and sausage gravy. Arthur could not get his fill, but he tried. Four days later, they departed the beach house for home, each with smiles to share.

Susan began her work with the research program and loved every minute of it. She excelled and was appointed as lead in most projects. The two-year period passed rapidly, providing important information to physicians treating the various forms of cancer. One month prior to the conclusion of her assignment, Susan was contacted by the National Institute of Health and offered a full-time position.

As she left the Stanford campus, she began to cry. So much of her life had happened here—the important part of her life.

On her drive across America, Susan decided to take advantage of the scenic spots. Her first stop was along the Snake River in Wyoming with a view of the Great Teton mountains. They did not disappoint. She photographed numerous wild animals from her car, visited Old Faithful, and considered learning to camp by a fire and enjoy Mother Nature. As she drove out of Yellowstone, she noticed numerous wild animals and concluded she was not a camper.

Her next stop was Colorado Springs and Pikes Peak. The idea of taking a trip up the mountain won her mind, and she entered that location in her GPS. As she drove toward Interstate 80, she was overcome again by the feeling of loneliness. She turned the car radio on as a distraction and immediately heard Kris Kristofferson sing *Loving Her Was The Easiest Thing I Have Ever Done*. Realizing that her view of relationships had been tainted by what she observed while at home watching her parents, she decided to open herself to men and to cultivate more positive connections.

Cassidy's name kept coming to mind, so she called him on her car radio. "You want to visit Pikes Peak with me?" she asked. "I'm in Cheyenne, Wyoming and headed south."

"What about Harry?" he asked. "He's more likely to put up with depressing discussions about cancer-stricken people."

"Cassidy, things have changed."

"Yes," he said. "Now you're an heiress, as well." He sounded bitter.

"You know I don't care about how much money you make. I make enough for both of us. Or will you ego prevent you from accepting my money?"

Frustrated, Susan stopped at a restaurant with a Western decor and reviewed the menu. While she was waiting for the hostess to seat her, a tall man wearing a cowboy hat and boots asked if she was alone for lunch.

"Yes," she said, thinking he could be a good diversion. "What's your name?"

"Derek Williston. And you?"

"Susan Howser."

The hostess seated them near a window.

"What's your favorite food," he asked when they had settled in.

"Raw meat and well-cooked veggies," she joked.

He looked surprised and then laughed. "So have you ever ridden a bull?"

"The two or four-legged kind?" she asked.

Again, taken aback, Derek replied, "Let us start with the four-legged ones."

Susan was becoming interested in the cowboy. He was well-mannered and witty. "Have you ever ridden a four-legged bull with horns?"

"Actually, yes. I'm a champion bull rider. You should come to the rodeo this afternoon. Be my guest."

Susan became excited about the event and agreed to attend. Derek suggested he wanted to fit her for a western blouse, a cowboy hat and boots. She was pleasantly surprised. When he stood to leave, Susan realized how tall he was.

They found the blouse, hat and boots at a local store near the restaurant. Susan noticed that Derek did not spend any money. When she started to pay the salesman, Derek said, "We do not owe anything. I am known as a Champion Bull Rider, which means free shopping in Cheyenne, Wyoming."

Susan asked, "What other benefits are there in Cheyenne when you are a celebrity?"

"Well," Derek replied, "I am not lonely. I love living here and being a single male."

Susan watched the rodeo from her vantage point along the fence at ground level. Derek's turn was the third bull out of the chute, and he came within about ten feet of Susan's seat. He rode his bull for the full eight seconds and then dismounted precisely in front of Susan's seat. He waved his hat to her.

When he came up to her in the seats, she hugged and kissed him as the crowd went wild. Susan had never experienced that type of adrenaline before. Derek picked her up and danced with her on the rodeo grounds, all the while waving to the crowd.

As they exited the arena, Derek told Susan that her first experience was just the beginning of the excitement. "Come with me to my apartment." She agreed.

As they entered, Susan knew the evening was going to be different than anything she'd experienced before. Without hesitation, Derek picked her up and carried her to a large bed. He placed her in the middle and started to remove the blouse they just purchased. Soon they were making love.

After five days and sleepless nights in Cheyenne, Susan concluded she was no longer lonesome. She had enjoyed a man more than she had ever before.

She left Cheyenne with a different outlook on her life and asked herself why she had lived twenty-four years with only a rare and somewhat disappointing experience at making love.

Unable to get Derek off of her mind, she called and asked him to join her in Maryland after she started her new job.

"Are there any rodeos there?" he asked.

"Probably not. How about a quick detour to Pikes Peak?"

Derek agreed to meet her there if Susan could pick him up at the airport.

Two weeks later, they parted ways. Susan was due at her new job, and Derek was scheduled for a rodeo in San Antonio, Texas.

"How much money will you make in San Antonio?"

"If I draw the right bull and stay on for eight seconds, I could net twenty-five thousand."

She replied, "You stayed on me longer than that, and you didn't make a cent."

Derek smiled. "Yes, but I will remember you forever."

***

Driving east on Interstate 70, Susan enjoyed the various scenic places that existed. Her mind shifted from one subject to another—Derek, her job, Derek, her investments, Derek again.

As she approached St. Louis, Missouri, she received a phone call from a representative of the National Institute of Health asking if she wanted to attend a four-day conference administered by the Mayo Clinic on childhood diseases. She agreed to attend provided her employer realized that this would delay her arrival.

During the conference, she was introduced by the conference chair as the student achieving the highest grade point as a graduate earning a doctorate in pediatric medicine from Stanford. Additionally, she had passed the bar in California. She was now en route to the National Institute of Health to focus her talents on preventing child hood diseases.

After the conference, Susan reported for work at the NIH and was warmly welcomed by a large group of fellow associates. She was introduced to a team of nine individuals who provided a brief synopsis of their background. Periodically, an associate asked a question which gave Susan the opportunity to elaborate on her own background.

One rather mature lady asked, "Are you married?"

"No, and I'm not planning to get married. I am committed to the advancement of improved health for young children, and that does not leave time for personal relationships."

"Well, that just leaves qualified men for the rest of us," the lady quipped.

Completing the introductions, Susan's host suggested the associates communicate their expectations of Susan's role as the leading expert on the program to be initiated at the NIH. She listened intently and asked if anyone would object if she recorded the discussions. Toward the end of the evening, an older, white-haired gentleman asked if she had begun to work on her original assignment at the NIH.

"No," she admitted, "however I have given many hours of thought to the subject of improved health for children. Once, in my younger life, I was responsible for two young ladies who were around ten years of age. They both died of an incurable cancer. I have not forgotten them, and I have committed my life's work to finding a cure for the disease that took their innocent lives." She took a moment to compose herself.

The white-haired gentleman remained standing. "Susan, I am pleased to welcome you to the effort I have also committed to for forty-five years—the cure of cancer. I lost my wife, two ten-year young twin girls, and one infant son. Someday, I would like to discuss our struggle. It gets lonesome with so few willing to take up the fight."

Susan replied, "Sir, this is unbearable." She started to cry and left the room but waited at the exit for the white-haired gentleman. When Susan saw him, she pulled him aside and hugged him.

"I'm Howard," he said, returning her hug. "I have no more tears, only a strong commitment to achieve my goal. I sense perhaps you can help me."

"I will do my best," Susan said.

She stopped by the lady's room and tried to wipe the tears from her eyes. As she looked in the mirror, she stood erect and prepared to meet her supervisor. She paused for a moment and thanked her Savior for his blessings and exited the lady's room.

As Susan entered the main office of the NIH, an attractive lady asked if she could assist her.

"Hi. I am Susan Howser, and I am here to see Dr. Graceland."

Dr. Graceland entered the room and introduced herself. She asked Susan to be seated.

"Mr. Greenwood couldn't be here, but he is a talented and motivated individual. I predict you will respect his achievements. I am confident your stay at the NIH will be rewarding for both you and the organization."

Dr. Graceland proceeded to explain her hopes for Susan's first thirty days of employment, including an in-depth orientation, mission statement, established goals, and a discussion of Susan's idea for the program she wanted to establish. As Dr. Graceland concluded her discussion, she informed Susan that her boss had asked to speak with her to discuss matters of common interest.

Susan asked for the director's cell phone number and assured Dr. Graceland she would establish appropriate contact. As they proceeded to Susan's office, she was pleasantly surprised to learn that it contained a large desk facing large windows that overlooked a scenic view of a garden. While she and Dr. Graceland were standing facing the windows, several colorful birds flew into the trees.

"Perfect," Susan said. "They arrived exactly as they were scheduled."

Dr. Graceland suggested that Susan continue to believe that was true.

Susan sat at her desk, adjusted the chair and made a list of items she wanted to have convenient to her as she performed assigned functions. She also called the director and invited him to join her at his convenience.

"Tomorrow at 9:00 a.m.?"

Susan agreed. Susan began to read the program on Preventing Childhood Cancer. Immediately, she began to shed tears as she thought of her two sweethearts.

Susan was assigned an administrative assistant. The chosen candidate would be shared by Susan and the VP of Personnel and Administrative Functions—Dr. Woodward. She was pleased to know that she would have help from someone familiar with the organization. More importantly, Susan was now in a position to achieve her primary goal—to find the cure that could have saved Caroline and Judith Ann.

www.ingramcontent.com/pod-product-compliance
Lightning Source LLC
Chambersburg PA
CBHW070652100726